JIMMY CARTER

CHAMPION OF PEACE

BY

ELLEN WEISS

★

AND

MEL FRIEDMAN

ALADDIN PAPERBACKS

New York   London   Toronto   Sydney   Singapore

First Aladdin Paperbacks edition January 2003

ALADDIN PAPERBACKS
An imprint of Simon & Schuster
Children's Publishing Division
1230 Avenue of the Americas
New York, NY 10020

Designed by Felicity Erwin
The text of this book was set in Adobe Garamond.

Printed in the United States of America
2 4 6 8 10 9 7 5 3 1

Library of Congress Control Number 2002115518
ISBN 0-689-86241-5

★CONTENTS★

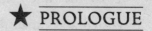 # PROLOGUE

On October 11, 2002, at about two minutes after four in the morning, the phone rang in Jimmy Carter's house in the tiny town of Plains, Georgia. "Please call the Nobel Prize Committee at four thirty," the caller instructed. For the next twenty-eight minutes, Carter and his wife, Rosalynn, were unsure whether the call was real or whether they were the victims of a hoax. While they knew it was a possibility that they would get this call one day, they had forgotten that this was the day it might actually come.

But it was real. Jimmy Carter had won the Nobel Peace Prize, the greatest and most respected honor in the world.

★ ★ ★

James Earl Carter came from virtually nowhere to become the thirty-ninth president of the United States. A peanut farmer and governor from the state of Georgia, he was close to unknown on the national scene until he ran for president in 1976. Often during his campaign he was greeted with the question, "Jimmy who?"

By the time Carter was elected, the country was disgusted and exhausted. Americans had been through a long and drawn-out war in Vietnam, which had gradually torn the country apart, killing almost sixty thousand American soldiers and more than a million Vietnamese for reasons that had become increasingly muddy. They had seen the resignation of Richard Nixon, whose presidency had been felled by a scandal known as Watergate. As the Watergate affair had unfolded, Nixon and his associates proved to have spied not only on their political opponents but on the American people as well. Nixon's vice president, Spiro Agnew, had already resigned because of his financial misdeeds, and by the time Nixon quit, the country had had enough of dirty politics.

Nixon's replacement, chosen by Nixon himself, was Gerald Ford. Ford seemed a reasonably able president, but his first official act in office was to issue a pardon to Richard Nixon, who otherwise would have had to stand trial. Though Ford's stated aim in issuing the pardon was to heal the country, the act caused many people to suspect that a deal had been made between

Nixon and his successor, with the pardon being the price of Ford's presidency. Whether or not this was the case, it left a cloud over Ford's otherwise unremarkable time in office.

And so when Jimmy Carter showed up out of nowhere to challenge Gerald Ford for the presidency, the country was ready for an "outsider", they wanted someone far removed from the scandal that had tainted national politics for nearly four years. And not only was Carter an outsider, but the country read him as an honest man. Carter promised the American people he would never lie to them, and this promise struck a deep chord. He talked about morals and values. And he was the first candidate to make an issue of human rights. "America," he said, "did not invent human rights. In a very real sense . . . human rights invented America."

Jimmy Carter also spoke unabashedly of being a born-again Christian. He talked about his Christianity in terms of inclusion and tolerance. "Carter," says political writer Hendrik Hertzberg, who worked as his speechwriter, "was the first and is still the only candidate for president who ever used the word 'love' . . . in virtually every campaign speech he delivered."

The country elected Jimmy Carter, but they let him stay for only one four-year term. He proved to be, as Hertzberg puts it, "an interesting experiment" for the United States. Carter's presidency was a mixed bag. He succeeded in a number of major achievements, most notably bringing together the leaders of Israel and Egypt, two countries that had been bitter enemies, to hammer out a lasting agreement for peace. But his term in office was also beset with disasters, some of which were not his fault. He was honest, but this honesty may have worked against him as often as it worked for him. He was not particularly good at public relations, and he became known—and mocked—as a nitpicker who got lost in the small details and could not see the big picture. In the end he was swept out of office by Ronald Reagan, who was perhaps the all-time master of public relations and who promised an eager-for-good-news country that it was "morning in America."

But then something unexpected happened. It was *after* he left office that Jimmy Carter became truly great. While most ex-presidents tend to content themselves with their private affairs, playing golf, or making money giving speeches, Carter got a gigantic second wind. "When I left the White House," he said, "I was a fairly young man and I realized I maybe have twenty-five more years of active life. So we capitalized on the influence that I had as a former president of the greatest nation in the world and decided to fill vacuums."

Carter became a whirlwind of energy, fighting to ensure better health and housing, and for democratic government for poor and oppressed people all over the world. With his wife, Rosalynn, he began tirelessly crossing the globe as a sort of freelance ambassador for peace—sometimes risking his own life to do so. He helped make sure that elections were held fairly in turbulent countries. He put out political fires by working behind the scenes to avert crises that could have led to war. Presidents have consulted with him often since he left office. He started the Carter Center, whose scholars, thinkers, doctors, scientists, and lawyers work to eradicate disease, stop wars, increase freedom, end hunger, and ease suffering all over the globe.

The Nobel Committee, based in Norway,

recognized all these achievements when it awarded Carter the prize, which comes with a million dollars—as well as enormous worldwide prestige. The committee's award statement carried a pointed message as the threat of a U.S. war against Iraq loomed on the horizon: "In a situation currently marked by threats of the use of power," said the statement, "Carter has stood by the principles that conflicts must as far as possible be resolved through mediation and international cooperation based on international law, respect for human rights, and economic development."

How did Jimmy Carter make the journey from a peanut farm in a tiny Southern town to winning the Nobel Prize? The answer lies in his origins. Just as his peanut plants put down deep roots in the red Georgia soil, so did Jimmy Carter.

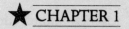

CHAPTER 1

CARTERS AND GORDYS

James Earl Carter Jr. was born on October 1, 1924, in the small farming community of Plains, Georgia—a town whose landscape was so unrelievedly flat, Carter recalls, that its residents would often joke, "When it rains, the water don't know which way to run."

Like so many small agricultural towns in early twentieth-century America, Plains evolved as a transportation and commercial crossroads for shipping local crops—cotton, peanuts, corn, peaches, watermelons, and potatoes—to distant urban markets and receiving processed and finished goods in return. Passenger and freight trains from the port city of Savannah chugged right through the heart of town, making daily stops at the depot and kicking up clouds of reddish dust that regularly settled down over the dozen or so two-story buildings that bordered Main Street.

The Plains of the 1920s supported a population of

several hundred and featured a grocery store (owned by Jimmy's father, James Earl Sr.), a bank, a café, a barber-shop, a post office, a drugstore, and a filling station. It was also home to one of southwest Georgia's most respected hospitals, the Wise Sanitarium, where Jimmy's mother, Bessie Lillian Gordy Carter, affectionately known as Miz Lillian, had studied and worked as a registered nurse. It was there that the future thirty-ninth president of the United States squallingly announced his arrival into the world. "I felt I had just become queen of the universe," his mother said of the event decades later, adding, "Not that he was anything to look at, of course. He was as ugly as any newborn. . . ." Although no one could have known it then, Jimmy Carter had already set a precedent of sorts. By sheer happenstance, he was on his way to becoming the first U.S. president ever born in a hospital.

The Carters of Plains—Jimmy's kinfolk on his father's side—had a rich, if turbulent, history. They were bright, enterprising souls, Southern Baptist by faith, with an uncanny knack for seizing opportunities and making money, as well as for becoming embroiled in minor squabbles that quickly escalated into murderous confrontations.

The family roots ran deep in American soil and were inextricably intertwined with the growth—and horrendous legacy—of slavery. Jimmy's paternal great-great-great-great-great-great-great-grandfather Thomas Carter was a colonist from England who built a homestead near the James River in Virginia in 1637.

One of Thomas Carter's descendants, Kindred Carter, stirred by wanderlust and dreams of vast, lush, cheap farmlands, pulled up stakes in the 1780s and moved to northeast Georgia. Kindred prospered and, at his death in 1800, left his heirs a sizable estate. By that time the practice of slaveholding—which, along with "demon" rum, Georgia had once banned as illegal and immoral—had become commonplace and firmly in place as a cornerstone of the state's economy. About two-thirds of the average Georgia plantation owner's wealth consisted of human "possessions"— abducted African slaves.

James Carter, one of Kindred's sons, found profit in slavery as well. He was a successful cotton grower who gradually expanded his holdings to more than four hundred acres and reportedly owned six slaves.

If Thomas Carter was the founding patriarch—the Abraham—of the Carters in America, James's son Wiley was their Moses, the person who led the family to the promised land. It was an exodus of necessity rather than of choice.

Wiley Carter fathered twelve children (all of whom lived, which was rare in those days) and was by all accounts a brilliant businessman and a strong-minded person. In 1843, at the age of forty-five, Wiley got into a bitter altercation with a man he accused of thievery. Guns were drawn, and, according to court testimony, Wiley fired in self-defense, killing his adversary. Although Wiley Carter was acquitted of any crime, the incident bitterly divided the community and persuaded Jimmy Carter's great-great-grandfather that it might be a good idea to relocate his family to safer, greener pastures.

Wiley chose a spot in the southwest corner of the state, just outside the growing agricultural village known as Plains of Dura—or Plains, for short. By 1858, the year his father, James, died, Wiley owned one of the largest plantations in the region. When Wiley himself died six years later, he was among the wealthiest ten percent of Georgians, leaving to his numerous heirs an estate that included more than a quarter of a million dollars in cash, twenty-four hundred acres of prize farmland, and forty-three slaves.

But Wiley Carter's golden touch when it came to commerce—his ability to reap extraordinary profits from his slave-driven plantation—could not protect his children and grandchildren from the violence that habitually threatened to explode in America's self-policed rural communities. In 1873 Littleberry Walker Carter, Wiley's eldest son and Jimmy's great-grandfather, was apparently knifed to death by a business partner over a trifle—the proceeds from the sale of a homemade merry-go-round.

In a gruesome replay of the tragedy Littleberry's son William Archibald Carter was gunned down thirty years later in a senseless dispute over claims to a desk. William's fifteen-year-old son, William Alton "Buddy" Carter, witnessed the shooting. "One bullet hit Daddy in the back of his head," Buddy would later recount. "We got the doctor and put Daddy on a train—we didn't have any automobiles then—and carried him to Cuthbert, where Mama was living. And he died there after being unconscious for a day or so."

William Carter—Jimmy Carter's grandfather—was survived by his wife, Nina, and his sons, Buddy and nine-year-old James Earl. In 1904 Buddy Carter, suddenly the man of the house, sold everything his father owned and moved the family into the town of Plains, where he formed a lucrative new business, the Plains Mercantile Company. The long-wandering Carter family, now headed by Jimmy Carter's uncle Buddy and his father, James Earl, were now the Carters of Plains, blown there by the dark winds of chance violence. It was an ambitious family composed of shrewd and gifted entrepreneurs who fit seamlessly into the South's overall system of economic and racial segregation.

★ ★ ★

The folks on Jimmy Carter's mother's side of the family—the Gordys—were of a different stripe entirely. They were mostly Methodists of liberal political outlook, descendants of Scottish immigrants to the

Mid-Atlantic states in the seventeenth century. As time went on, the Gordys developed a tradition of involvement in the political life of their home state.

Peter Gordy III, Jimmy Carter's great-great-great-grandfather, brought the Gordys to central Georgia in the early nineteenth century. During the Civil War, James Thomas Gordy fought with the Georgia State Militia and served as a local tax collector. One of his sons, Francis Marion Gordy, became a doctor, was elected county clerk several times, and twice won election to the Georgia State Senate. But it was a second son, James Jackson Gordy (named after James Jackson, a Georgia Revolutionary War hero), who would figure more directly in the political education and philosophy of the young Jimmy Carter.

Jim Jack, as James Gordy was called, was Jimmy Carter's maternal grandfather. He was originally a teacher in a one-room schoolhouse that he built himself. But his true passion was politics and working in the smoke-filled back rooms where election strategies were typically hatched and political fortunes determined. Unlike his brother Francis Marion, Jim

Jack never ran for office himself. But he did hold a number of patronage jobs, posts that were handed out as rewards for political support or contributions. These jobs included a longtime stint as postmaster in the town of Richland, about twenty miles west of Plains, and a comfortable spot as doorkeeper at the state capitol in Atlanta.

In his memoirs Jimmy Carter recalls his grandfather as a restless man who never seemed able to muster much affection for any of his family members apart from his daughter, Jimmy's mother, Bessie Lillian. Instead he preferred to channel all his passion and energy into the subjects he loved most: election campaigns, party gossip, and political intrigue.

Jimmy Carter describes Jim Jack as "a man's man . . . tall, slender, handsome, and always well groomed and neatly dressed." But his distinguishing characteristic, Carter writes, was his political shrewdness: "Our family was always proud of Grandpa's ability to predict local election results. He would write down the expected returns on election eve, put them in a sealed envelope, and give them to the county clerk to retain. When opened after the results were known, they always turned out to be remarkably accurate," often within five votes.

Carter notes that his uncle Buddy, thinking back on that period, could not recall a single election in which Jim Jack had not played an important role. As one of Jimmy Carter's biographers, James Wooten, confirms, Jim Jack "never ran for office himself, but he manipulated the fortunes of those in the area who did."

Although Jim Jack's political positions were often hard to predict—and, some say, self-serving and opportunistic—his basic impulses were progressive, liberal, and populist. His unabashed political idol was Tom Watson, a Georgia congressman who had been booted out of the Democratic Party for suggesting that blacks and whites be entitled to equal economic treatment, a shocking idea at the time. Jim Jack was not a personal friend of Watson's but did have correspondence with him.

As sometimes happens, though, in the fierce cockpit of public life, Watson's political path took a bizarre and ugly turn. Ostracized as a Democrat, he joined the newly formed Populist Party and ran for office three times, once for vice president and twice for president. After losing all three bids Watson became embittered and underwent an appalling political metamorphosis. He rejected his long-standing liberalism and won a U.S. Senate seat by campaigning on a viciously anti-Catholic, anti-Semitic, and anti-black platform.

Tom Watson remained Jim Jack's hero to the end—throughout all the repellent twists and turns of Watson's political philosophy. Jim Jack even named one of his sons, Tom Watson Gordy, after the once-great champion of the working man. But it is unlikely that Jim Jack ever embraced the bigoted dogmas of segregation and racism that characterized the latter part of Watson's career. Jim Jack maintained a warm friendship with a prominent black community leader, Bishop William Johnson of the African Methodist Episcopal Church, and he made no attempt to disguise this fact. He was not even afraid to receive Bishop Johnson in his home, a flagrant violation of the taboos of segregation in those days. His daughter Lillian once pointedly remarked that Tom Watson may have hated blacks, but "my father did not." In her view her father was an inclusive person and a liberal on the subject of race, someone who preached tolerance and passed this value on to her and, through her, to her son Jimmy.

The natures of Jimmy Carter's two ancestral clans, then, could hardly have been more different. The Carters were a long line of farmers with a genius for finding and exploiting business opportunities where none had existed before. They were not self-doubting or overly reflective people. They did not stop to question their lives or ponder the moral legitimacy of a system based on racial exploitation. The Gordys, on the other hand, were mostly townsfolk, more cosmopolitan in outlook. They were not drawn to the soil like the Carters, nor did they seem to have any special aptitude for commerce. What they did have, though, was a deep appreciation for the value of learning and a passionate interest in politics.

At birth Jimmy Carter was endowed with the best traits of both families. He would prove to have a keen business mind as well as a growing instinct for fairness and justice. The Gordy side dominated in one key area, though. As Carter scholar Kenneth Morris has noted, "Politically, Jimmy Carter would mature very much a Gordy—the product of his mother's and grandfather's influence—more so than a Carter." Jim Jack had believed that politics could be a force for moral change, and so would his grandson.

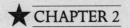 **CHAPTER 2**

THE OUTSIDER

Jimmy Carter's boyhood had a profound effect on his moral, spiritual, and political development. It provided him with strong role models. It influenced his thinking on matters of race relations, human rights, and the unfulfilled promise of American democracy. It set him on his chosen career path: a life in the navy. It drew him back to Plains after his father died. And it instilled in him the values that propelled him into politics, once he concluded that public service was the most meaningful way for him to make a difference in people's lives.

In many respects, Jimmy Carter's formative experiences were different from those of any other president—before or since. He was a child of affluence who grew up among poor black tenant farmers. The children of those farmers were his constant companions, and he counted some of them as among his most important early role models.

His father, James Earl Sr. (everyone called him Earl), was a generous-spirited, larger-than-life figure who was well liked by everyone—blacks as well as whites—despite his strongly held segregationist views. Jimmy Carter saw his dad as "the center of my life and the focus of my admiration when I was a child. He was a serious and sometimes stern businessman, but often lively and full of fun with his friends and with the men and women who lived on our farm." As a parent, though, Earl could be cold and emotionally aloof. He demanded excellence and absolute obedience from his children but rarely gave praise. "You're not better than anyone, and no one else is better than you" was his often repeated motto.

"It was not natural for my father to admit a mistake," Carter writes, "and as a child I was inclined to consider him omniscient and infallible." Earl's nickname for his son Jimmy was Hot, short for Hotshot. Carter notes wistfully, "I never remembered him saying, 'Good job, Hot,' or thanking me when I had done my best to fulfill one of his quiet suggestions that had the impact of orders." As Carter once told an interviewer, "Daddy never assumed that I would fail at anything."

For Earl Carter failure was not simply a dirty word—it was a totally alien concept. Earl had inherited the Carter genes for being in the right place at the right time with the right goods. When he died in 1953, his net worth was variously estimated between a quarter of a million and a million dollars, a princely sum back in those days. Even so, his tireless work habits, his frugality, and his lack of ostentation made it unlikely that his son Jimmy ever felt especially rich or privileged as he was growing up. Jimmy's boyhood living conditions, while not as relentlessly harsh as he has sometimes made them out to be, were nonetheless far from the comfortable circumstances of a typical child of wealth—or even the modest circumstances of a 1920s lower-middle-class urban child.

Jimmy was the firstborn of Earl and Lillian Carter's four children. His sisters, Gloria and Ruth, were born in 1926 and 1929, respectively, and his brother, William Alton II, in 1937. In 1928, when Jimmy was four years old, his father transplanted the family from tiny Plains to the still-tinier town of Archery, about two and a half miles away. Earl had the foresight to buy 350 acres of the last good farmland in the area with the intention of raising a variety of cash crops and opening an agricultural supply warehouse and a general store.

Until this move Jimmy's whole world was centered in Plains, where white folks and black folks never mixed and where the comparatively prosperous Carters were regarded as the town's "first family." In isolated Archery, however, the situation changed radically. The Carters were in the minority—one of only two white families in a relatively impoverished community of more than two dozen black households. Some of the black families lived in small clapboard houses on the Carter property, where the men were employed as tenant farmers for Earl and the women as household help. Thrown together in this way the whites and blacks of Archery needed to interact frequently and get along well, if only for social harmony and economic self-interest.

For the next ten years Jimmy's playmates and best friends were almost exclusively black children—the sons of his father's tenant farmers. As a result Jimmy Carter spent most of his free time in black homes, playing with his black friends, and acquiring practical skills from the handful of black adults who were designated to serve as Jimmy's surrogate parents when his father was busy with the farm and his mother was away nursing others.

The psychological impact of this blurring of the lines of racial separation was significant. Jimmy Carter writes that it made him aware of his otherness. He often felt like the person who didn't belong—like a white "outsider" looking in on a black child's world. To the extent that he was conscious of this racial divide he strove mightily to fit in better by emulating the behavior of the black children in his neighborhood. More than anyone else in his family, Carter says, "I could understand the plight of the black families, because I lived so much among them." Then he adds poignantly, "My own life was shaped by a degree of personal intimacy between black and white people that is now almost completely unknown and largely forgotten." Except for his own parents, he says, of the five or six people "who most deeply affected my early life," only two were white.

But in the 1920s and 1930s—the heyday of the Jim Crow laws that enforced racial inequality in the South—Jimmy Carter had neither the mental maturity nor the approval of society to imagine any alternative to the way things were. Segregation was an unquestioned way of life. When Jimmy and his black friend A. D. wanted to see a movie "together," for example, they had to travel by train in a segregated coach car to nearby Americus. Carter was allowed to sit in the front; A. D. had to sit in the rear. When they exited the train, the two friends would reunite and walk together to the theater, chatting normally. At the theater they would separate again to watch the film in their respective white and colored sections. "Afterward," Carter relates, "we would go back home, united in friendship though physically divided on the segregated train. Our only strong feeling was one of gratitude for our wonderful excursion; I don't remember ever questioning the mandatory racial separation, which we accepted like breathing or waking up in Archery every morning." It would be years before Carter would recognize the folly and bankruptcy of a system that forced friends and neighbors to live in separate and unequal parallel worlds.

Jimmy Carter's childhood coincided with the period of the Great Depression, which shook the foundations of rural America long before it toppled the stock market in 1929. Paradoxically the depression had a positive effect on Earl Carter's fortunes, because it lowered his labor costs. With his usual shrewdness Earl Carter also anticipated a rising demand for peanuts. In Alabama, George Washington Carver had for years been doing his incredible research on peanuts at the Tuskeegee Institute, developing more than three hundred uses for them, including peanut butter. Carver single-handedly transformed peanuts from a crop that nobody grew to the second largest cash crop—after cotton—in the South. Most of the work on Earl Carter's farm, of course, was performed by African-American hands and sharecroppers, who were paid very little. But even with all the available help and the slow but steady growth of Earl Carter's cash box, daily life on the Archery homestead was rather simple. The Carters had no running water in their three-bedroom clapboard farmhouse until Jimmy was eleven. Prior to that time they "drew water from a well in the yard," Carter recalls, "and every day of the year we had the chore of keeping extra bucketfuls in the kitchen and on the back porch." In place of a toilet every bedroom had its own slop jar, or chamber pot, which was emptied each morning into the outdoor privy, about twenty yards from the back door. The outhouse itself was the height of extravagance. It was equipped with "a large hole for adults and a lower and smaller one for children" as well as a stack of "old newspapers or pages torn from Sears, Roebuck catalogues" for sanitary purposes.

The house had no electricity, either, until Jimmy Carter was a teenager, when a special federal government program, the Rural Electrification Administration, finally strung power lines to millions of American farm homes that had been living in the dark ages. The absence of electricity during Jimmy's childhood meant that his house had no oil burners, no electric heat, no electric lights, no electric appliances, no plug-in record players or radios (the Carters did have a battery-powered radio), and, for a while, no telephone service. Because Jimmy's bedroom was in the rear of the house, far from any sources of heat, he often went to bed in the wintertime with heated bricks slipped under his covers for warmth. After-dark reading in the Carter household—the favorite indoor pastime of Jimmy, his siblings, and his book-loving mother—all occurred under the faint glow of kerosene lamps.

Food was always plentiful. Corn was the Carters' staple grain at mealtime. Rarely was a dish prepared without an accompanying side of grits, lye hominy, roasting ears, or corn bread. "We always had chickens available, either hens or fryers," Carter remembers, "and it was usually my job to catch and kill them so they could be dressed and then baked, fried, or made into a pie for dinner or supper." Fresh vegetables usually included peas, potatoes, string beans, butter beans, okra, rutabagas, and collard greens. "We also had mashed Irish potatoes or rice and gravy, biscuits, and a pie made from seasonal fruit or sweet potatoes." Perishables were kept from spoiling by a kitchen icebox that was regularly replenished with cold blocks by a door-to-door iceman.

Like most farm folk in rural Georgia, Jimmy Carter went barefoot through all but the coldest winter months. He didn't routinely begin wearing shoes until about the age of thirteen, when etiquette dictated that he put on shoes for church and school.

Jimmy was also responsible for performing various daily and seasonal chores. As a young child he would tote water to the waiting field hands at sunup. Later, when he was of school age, he would chop and saw wood for the kitchen stove and two fireplaces and rekindle the stove before setting out on his daily two-mile trek to class in Plains. At night his job was often to make sure that all the kerosene lamps were filled with oil. Sometimes Jimmy's father would ask him for help in shoeing the mules and horses, sharpening plowpoints, repairing machinery, and forging simple iron implements. Beyond that there was the typical backbreaking farmwork, including harvesting and stacking peanuts and cotton, and shocking and threshing wheat, oats, and rye. Occasionally Jimmy would have to help his father both before *and* after school—and sometimes all day on Saturday.

Still, Jimmy Carter's life on the farm wasn't all work. As Jimmy grew older and Earl's wealth increased, so did the family's consumption. "We weren't rich, but we weren't poor," Miz Lillian once explained to a reporter. "We lived very, very well in terms of having what we needed—and a little bit more." Under the category of "a little bit more" were such luxuries as a piano, a large record collection, a Ping-Pong table, a horse for Jimmy, a pool table, bicycles, dolls, toys, hunting and fishing gear, a tennis court (built by Earl and Jimmy), a pond and pond house (both constructed by Earl), a jukebox, a succession of expensive cars, and books, books, and more books.

But Earl did not confine his generosity to his family. In the spirit of Christian charity—as much as to avoid embarrassing people he knew—he liked to donate money anonymously to deserving families and causes. His kindness extended to blacks as well. He was what some might have termed a softhearted segregationist, someone who wouldn't dream of inviting a black man into his home but who would build by hand a beautiful silk-lined casket for a black infant who had died, weeping uncontrollably as he worked. Earl was the one who underwrote all the expenses of the free medical care Miz Lillian provided to the black community. His black workers also knew that they could count on him for loans and handouts without any questions asked.

Thus Jimmy Carter's childhood gave him unique insights into the lives and concerns of black Americans who were suffering under segregation. He was able to identify in himself similar feelings of isolation and alienation, which were the beginnings of authentic empathy. With education and greater exposure to the outside world Jimmy Carter would begin putting all the intellectual pieces together for himself. He would wholeheartedly reject the racist narrowness of his father and embrace the compassionate liberalism of his mother.

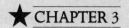

CHAPTER 3

THE LARGER WORLD

From an early age Jimmy showed that he had a good head for business as well as for schoolwork. "I began selling boiled peanuts on the streets of Plains when I was five years old," he recollects. "This was my first acquaintance with the outside world." At harvesttime he would uproot the peanut vines, load them into a little red wagon, and haul them home. Then he would separate and clean the nuts and let them soak overnight in salted water. The next day he would boil the peanuts in salt water, remove them from the bath, and, after they had cooled, dump them into half-pound paper bags, which he would load into his wagon and drag two and a half miles into Plains. There he would sell his bags for a nickel apiece. "I had some regular customers who would buy about half my peanuts every day and seemed grateful for them," Carter says. When sales were brisk, he earned about one dollar per weekday and about five dollars on Saturdays. Peanuts were to remain the primary source of Carter's income for the bulk of the next forty-eight years.

Jimmy launched other successful moneymaking ventures as well. At various times he partnered with his cousin Hugh to sell hamburgers and hot dogs on Main Street (a nickel each), ice cream outside the bank (three scoops for a nickel), old newspapers to a fish market for wrapping fish, and scrap iron for salvage (twenty cents per hundred pounds).

By the age of nine Jimmy had saved enough money to purchase five bales of cotton, which were going cheap due to the depression. His father, Earl, advised him to store the cotton until prices rose. Jimmy listened. Four years later, when the market improved, he sold his cotton for triple what he'd paid. With the earnings Jimmy bought five tenant houses from a local mortician and quickly rented each one out for $16.50 a month. At thirteen Earl Carter's son had become a profitable landlord! Jimmy Carter continued receiving rental income from these properties up through the middle of World War II.

Both Earl Carter and his wife, Lillian, put a heavy emphasis on the value of education for their children. Following the murder of his father Earl had dropped out of school before reaching the ninth grade, and he was determined that his children would do better. In fact he demanded nothing less than perfection. "No mark was ever good enough," Jimmy's sister Gloria recalls. "If we got ninety-seven, Daddy would say, 'Why didn't you make a hundred?' If we got a B we were sentenced to dig ditches. He was never happy with our grades."

Miz Lillian exerted a softer but probably more lasting influence on Jimmy's love of learning. An insatiable reader, she encouraged her children to follow her example. Unlike most households, at mealtimes the Carter household was totally silent. Everyone—Miz Lillian, Jimmy, his siblings—read at the table with the exception of Earl, who had trouble with his eyesight.

When Jimmy Carter started first grade in Plains at the age of six, he was already able to read and write. At the time all white children in Georgia were required to attend schools, then segregated, at least until they turned sixteen. Jimmy quickly found ways to balance his farm and school obligations. When he wasn't doing chores, Carter writes, "I usually had a book with me, and read on rainy days, Sunday afternoons, in bed at night, at the table during meals, in my tree house, on the toilet, and between and even during classes at school." His zeal was so great that his second and third grade teachers awarded him a prize for reading the most books of his peers.

By all accounts Jimmy was an exceptional student if not a stellar athlete (sports participation was mandatory for boys) or an overtly political animal. In all his public school years he never held a single elected class office! The Plains public school system was tiny. It had fewer than three hundred students in eleven grades. The total number of students in Carter's high school graduating class—twenty-six—could fit comfortably in one room. Of those twenty-six Carter was the only one who went on to college after graduation in 1941.

One of Jimmy Carter's former classmates later recalled him as being "the smartest in the class," a statement borne out by the fact that he received straight

As in every subject except music and physical education and graduated at the top of his class. History, literature, and music were among his favorite subjects. Jimmy ran track and also played forward on the basketball team. He wasn't an outstanding shooter, but he made up for it with spunk and speed. "I was by far the smallest one on the team," Carter remembers, and his teammates dubbed him Peewee, after a popular comic-strip character. "But I was also the quickest," he adds, which benefited the team a lot because it relied on fast breaks whenever it got the ball on the opponents' end of the court.

Another classmate, who served with Carter on the high school debate team, recalls, "his facts and material were always tops, and he could give you quick references, but his delivery wasn't tops."

"He wasn't shy," his sister Gloria once told a reporter. "He was little. He was only five foot three when he went away to college. He was always wondering if he'd ever grow." He did—to five foot nine—during his first year in college.

It is telling that one of the individuals Jimmy

Carter has always singled out as having a life-changing influence on him was his high school English teacher, Miss Julia Coleman. "She was the best teacher I have ever had," Carter writes. "She walked with a limp, had failing eyesight, and never raised her voice to scold or in anger; her only marriage was to our school. She was totally dedicated to her profession. . . ." Carter attributes his lifelong love of classical literature, art, and music to this extraordinary teacher, who prescribed his reading lists and gave him "a silver star for every five books" he read and "a gold star for ten book reports" he wrote. More than three decades later Carter took the remarkable step of paying tribute to his beloved former teacher in his inaugural address as president of the United States.

In 1935, while he was still a grammar school student, Jimmy Carter was baptized into the First Baptist Church of Plains, a conservative and evangelical denomination. Religion was a regular and important part of Carter family life. Jimmy's father, Earl, was a deacon in the Plains Baptist church, where he also taught Sunday-school classes. Jimmy's sister Ruth would one day became a famous evangelist. And Jimmy himself, as a child and as an adult, studied theology. He would later declare himself a born-again Christian and become a deacon and a Sunday-school teacher in the same Plains church in which his father served.

Before he was even a first-grader, Jimmy Carter knew exactly what he wanted to do in life: He wanted to become a U.S. naval officer and see the world. Jimmy had two important role models to follow. His father, Earl, had enlisted in the U.S. Army in 1916 as a private and served with distinction in World War I, reaching the rank of lieutenant. Another and more decisive influence was Jimmy's uncle Tom Watson Gordy, his mother's brother, who had joined the navy at a young age and had made a lifetime career of it.

During Jimmy's formative years he and his uncle Tom maintained a lively correspondence. "He was my distant hero," Carter writes, "and through all the years of my boyhood, he and I wrote letters back and forth"— Carter's communications filled with family news and Uncle Tom's "filled with information about the exotic places his ships were visiting" across the world's wide oceans. Jimmy began to dream of having a life like Tom's. From the time he was five, Carter relates, "I would always say that someday I would be going to Annapolis and would become a naval officer." Indeed, years before he graduated from high school, he had written to the U.S. Naval Academy at Annapolis, Maryland, asking for information on its entrance requirements. "I adopted this as my exclusive goal in life."

Carter knew that the admission standards at Annapolis were extremely competitive and there were many reasons why a prospective applicant might be disqualified, one of which was flat feet—which he had. So, in order to pass the academy's rigorous physical entrance requirements, Carter rolled his feet on Coke bottles every day until he developed an artificial arch.

In the two years following his graduation from high school in 1941 Carter attended Georgia Southwestern College in nearby Americus, and then the Georgia Institute of Technology in Atlanta, where he studied nuclear engineering and enrolled in Naval ROTC. While at Georgia Tech, Carter's boyhood dream came true: He received an appointment to Annapolis.

In 1943 Carter, just shy of nineteen years old, enrolled in the U.S. Naval Academy. It was the middle of War World II.

Carter excelled in electronics, gunnery, and naval tactics and graduated in 1946, ranking fifty-ninth in a class of 820. Upon leaving Annapolis he served two years in the navy, chiefly as an electronics instructor. In 1952 Carter signed on with a special group of officers who were developing the world's first nuclear-powered submarines under the leadership of the "father" of atomic submarines, Captain Hyman Rickover. Carter was made engineering officer of the nuclear submarine *Sea Wolf,* which was under Rickover's command. Carter later told an interviewer, "Rickover was a man who demanded absolute excellence and total dedication from all those who worked under him. He demanded as much from himself. And so, he set a standard of commitment and perfection in life that I had never experienced before. He really had a great impact on my life."

On a visit to Plains before his last year at Annapolis, Jimmy Carter met Rosalynn Smith, a friend of his sister Ruth's, who had once lived next door to the Carter house in Plains. Rosalynn was only seventeen years old at the time, three years Jimmy's junior. They dated and then corresponded when Jimmy returned to the Academy. Jimmy was smitten with her and told his mother almost immediately, "She's the one I want to marry." Jimmy proposed marriage, but Rosalynn demurred, saying she wasn't quite ready yet. The second time Jimmy asked, she said yes. The two were married in July of 1946. Their first son John William (Jack) was born in the following year. Jimmy and Rosalynn would eventually have two more sons—James Earl III (Chip) was born in 1950, and Donnel Jeffrey was born in 1952—and a daughter, Amy Lynn, who arrived in 1967.

Carter was extremely happy in the navy, even though he had to work long hours. As many wives did in those days, Rosalynn stayed home and cared for the children. A newly commissioned lieutenant, Jimmy Carter seemed to have a brilliant military career ahead of him. But fate had other plans in mind for the young Georgian and his new family.

CHAPTER 4

RETURN TO THE PEANUT FARM

Just as his navy career seemed headed securely upward, something happened that would change Jimmy Carter's life forever. His father, who had just been elected to the Georgia State Legislature, became ill with cancer. Carter asked for leave from his job on the nuclear submarine and went home to spend some precious time with his father. At that point he and Rosalynn had three young boys.

While he was home, Carter began to get a better understanding of what his father had meant to the community of Plains. Earl Carter's life had touched those of everyone around him. "One woman," Rosalynn recalled, "said her husband had gotten sick and died back in the early thirties when nobody had any money, and Jimmy's father brought her twenty-five dollars a month for over two years. That was a lot of money back then, and she said if he hadn't done that, they couldn't have lived. They were destitute. His father was really a great man." Earl had even bought graduation dresses for girls who could not afford them so that they could graduate from high school without feeling humiliated.

Earl Carter died in July of 1953, and Jimmy made a decision. He would move back home with his family, run the farm, and take up where his father had left off. "I saw," he said later, "that my daddy's life was very valuable to people." This revelation made Jimmy Carter feel that he could be of much more service to people from the base of his hometown than he could ever be in the navy.

Rosalynn hated this idea. She had gotten used to traveling, and she loved seeing the world. And she could not understand why her husband would want to give up a promising navy career to go home and be a peanut farmer.

"I argued. I cried. I even screamed at him," she said later. "I loved our life in the navy and the independence I had finally achieved. I knew it would be gone if we went home to live in the same community with my mother and Jimmy's mother. Plains had too many ghosts for me."

Carter agrees that it was a bad time. "It was the first really serious argument in our marriage," he wrote. He even told an interviewer, years later, that Rosalynn had almost left him. But finally Carter prevailed. He resigned from the navy with the rank of lieutenant senior grade, and the Carters moved back to Plains to start a new life with their three boys.

They did not have an easy time of it. Carter had to remember or relearn what he knew about peanut farming; he had been away for a long time. And on top of that they had a drought to contend with their first year home. After their first season, they had earned a meager $187.

But Jimmy Carter was a man who knew the value of education, so he went back to school to study modern farming methods at the University of Georgia Agricultural Experiment Station in Tifton, Georgia. Rosalynn began taking care of the farm's bookkeeping, the rains finally came, the warehouse filled up, and life got better.

Carter did not just follow his father in the running of the farm—he literally stepped into his father's shoes. He joined the library and hospital boards and the

Sumter County School Board, the same boards his father had served on. Like his father, Carter also became a deacon and a Sunday-school teacher at the Plains Baptist church. Jimmy even liked to wear Earl's old World War I boots when he went quail hunting, to the amusement of his friends.

This was a difficult time of transition for the South. The segregation laws that had restricted blacks' access to schools, stores, drinking fountains, and bus seats were starting to come under attack, both in the streets and in the courts. In May of 1954 the United States Supreme Court decided that the segregation of schools was unconstitutional. White Southerners were outraged at this threat to the way of life they had always known, and they fought back. An organization called the White Citizens' Council was formed to combat integration, and in 1955 a chapter was started in Plains. Jimmy Carter, who was opposed to segregation, was the only white man in the town who refused to join it. It took enormous courage to fly in the face of his neighbors' anger, and it was lonely. Their peanut business was boycotted, but Jimmy and

Rosalynn stood firm. Eventually the boycott petered out.

Carter was on the local school board, and he was committed to seeing the schools integrated, both as a matter of law and as a matter of morality. "Some of the major politicians in Georgia," he recalled in an interview, "even though they were looked upon as being moderate, were promising that if one black child went into the public school system, they would close it down. The leading candidate for governor had a slogan: 'No, not one,' and he would hold up one finger to indicate this. So I decided that I could protect the school system if I went to the Georgia Senate."

In typical fashion Carter kept this decision to himself. Rosalynn did not know he was thinking about running, she recalled, "until he got up on his thirty-seventh birthday on October first in 1961 and put on slacks instead of the khakis which he always wore to the warehouse and I said, 'Where are you going?' and he said, 'I'm going to Americus to see who's going to run for the state senate.' He came back home and said no one from Sumter County was going to run for the senate and asked me what I thought about it, and I thought it was great. I was all for it. But that was the first time I ever knew he was thinking about it."

The first hurdle to be gotten over was the primaries. These are the first elections that are held for each party to narrow the group of candidates down to the two candidates who will face off in the general election. It was during the primaries that Carter had an eye-opening introduction to Georgia state politics. Observing the voting in the town of Georgetown, he noticed that people were casting votes right under the eyes of the poll supervisors, a clear violation of the law. A universal principle of fair voting is that it is supposed to be secret, so that no one can be intimidated into voting for a particular candidate. When Carter protested, he was ignored.

Carter lost the Democratic primary by just a few votes. But by now he was really furious, and he was not going to accept the results without a fight. He got a newspaper in Atlanta interested in the issue of voter fraud throughout the state, and he also fought the outcome in court. It was determined that the ballot boxes had been stuffed with votes for his opponent—

votes supposedly cast by people who were dead, in prison, or not registered to vote. The local powers did not go down without a fight. Carter and his family were followed and threatened. Though it was terrifying, they persevered, and just three days before the general election, Carter was judged to be the winner and placed on the ballot, although it was so late that in some places people had to write in his name. He won that election by about a thousand votes.

Carter remained true to his goal of working to improve the educational prospects of all Georgians, black or white. "When I was finally elected and got to Atlanta," he recalled, "my only request to the Senate was to be put on the Education Committee, and I very quickly became the chairman of the University Committee." Carter quickly gained the respect of his fellow lawmakers, becoming known as an independent and tough-minded legislator. In addition to being dedicated to education issues, he was fiercely committed to eliminating waste in government spending and worked effectively to trim the budget. In 1964, at the end of his first term as state senator, he was reelected.

In 1966 Carter decided to move higher, and he announced his candidacy for the House of Representatives. But when a longtime Republican rival decided to switch his candidacy from that race to the race for governor of Georgia, Carter switched as well. But he quickly hit a wall. In a Georgia still reeling from the rapid change that forced integration had brought, a liberal Democrat did not stand much of a chance. Carter did not even win the primary, finishing a dismal third. The winner of that year's general election turned out to be one Lester Maddox, who won national celebrity by brandishing an ax handle for reporters and distributing replicas to his supporters. The ax handles were a symbolic way to bring home the message that he would never, ever allow black people into the restaurant he owned, despite the fact that the Civil Rights Act of 1964 required him to serve them. Up North, Maddox was seen as a sort of Stone Age remnant of the Old South, but in the Georgia of 1966 he was a hero to many.

Carter took his defeat hard. He was not used to losing. "It was the first real defeat in my life," he recalled in an interview. "Whenever I wanted something in the navy, I got it because I was an outstanding officer. I worked hard. So that was a very serious blow to me. I was very distressed. And my sister Ruth Stapleton was a famous evangelist; she wrote four or five books, and she gave lectures to fifty thousand people at a time. She and I had a long walk in the woods on my farm, and she said, 'Jimmy, quite often . . . when you have a blow to your pride and a horrible defeat, you can either give up, or you can look on it as a way that God opens you to do different and even better things.' And I said, 'Ruth, I've been defeated for governor in Georgia; my political career is over. I don't have any future.' But that proved to be wrong."

It proved to be wrong because Carter decided to run again in 1970, and this time he had a very different approach to running his campaign. In a strategy that would foreshadow the methods he has used into the twenty-first century, he apparently decided that he would make any compromise necessary to attain the position in which he could achieve his real goals. If Jimmy Carter was going to win, he would have to gather the votes of all those who had voted for Maddox four years before. And so Carter reinvented his image. Gone was Carter's outspoken opposition to segregation. Gone were his forward-thinking speeches. Now he said nice things about Lester Maddox and about Alabama governor George Wallace, who in 1963 had stood in the doorway of the University of Alabama to block black students from enrolling there until the National Guard finally forced him to move aside. Carter made a visit to a segregated private school and told the crowd at a rally not to "let anybody, including the Atlanta newspapers, mislead you into criticizing private education." He even asked for the endorsement of Lester Maddox, who was not running again because he was limited to one term. By the time he had finished remaking his image, Carter had done such an effective job that the *Atlanta Constitution*, the state's most influential newspaper, would not endorse him. They called him an "ignorant, racist, backward, ultra-conservative, red-necked South Georgia peanut farmer."

Carter won the election. And then at his inauguration he pulled a surprise on everyone. "I say to you quite frankly," he said in his speech, "that the time for racial discrimination is over. No poor, rural, weak, or black person should ever have to bear the additional burden of being deprived of the opportunity of an education, a job, or simple justice." This speech was so unusual that the entire nation sat up and paid attention.

He was as good as his word too. He immediately began working extraordinarily hard to achieve the goals that were dear to him. He pushed the legislature to pass a law that restructured state aid to schools, equalizing the amounts given to the state's wealthy and poor areas. He introduced "sunshine laws," which made the secretive workings of the state government open and accessible to its citizens. He established community centers for mentally disabled children. He set up educational programs for prison inmates. He protected large areas of Georgia wilderness for the generations to come. He made sure that judges and state government officials were appointed on the basis of merit, rather than by who their political allies were.

He also opened the state government more than ever before to African Americans. While he was governor, Jimmy Carter increased the number of black appointees to major state posts from three to fifty-three. He formed biracial committees to address racial issues. During Carter's administration, the number of black state employees went from 4,850 to 6,684.

True to his long-standing passion, he paid a lot of attention to streamlining the state government so that it would run more smoothly and cost less to operate. He consolidated three hundred agencies that often competed and overlapped into twenty-two "super-agencies." During this process he displayed the near-obsessive attention to detail that would eventually work against him as president. He also frequently antagonized the old-time political figures in the state and gained a reputation as being abrasive and somewhat holier-than-thou.

Perhaps the most important symbolic thing that Carter did during his term in office involved the portraits that hung in the statehouse. The halls were lined with portraits of Georgia dignitaries, but not one of those dignitaries was black. Carter appointed a commission to study the problem, and they recommended that a portrait of Dr. Martin Luther King Jr., who came from Georgia, be hung on the wall. In 1974 the picture went up—despite discouragement from Carter's friends and advisers, and despite the fact that angry citizens, including the Ku Klux Klan, demonstrated in the street in front of the capitol.

Because he was limited to one term, Carter was already devoting thought to what he would do next. In the course of his governorship he had had contact with many high-ranking politicians from across the country and over time became convinced that he was just as qualified to run for the highest office in the country as they were. He also had a hunch that the nation's voters would be receptive to someone completely fresh, someone who came from far outside Washington. He began to think about running for the presidency in 1976.

One day in September 1973 his mother, Miz Lillian, asked him what he was thinking about doing after being governor. "I'm going to run for president," he replied. "President of what?" she asked. "Momma," he said, "I'm going to run for president of the United States, and I'm going to win."

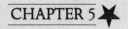

CHAPTER 5

JIMMY WHO?

Jimmy Carter knew he had a tough road ahead if he was going to make it to the White House. Outside of Georgia not many people knew who he was, even though as governor he had been featured on the cover of *Time* magazine as the face of the New South. In fact he had appeared on the television show *What's My Line* and stumped the panel, which was supposed to guess what their mystery guest did for a living. The day after he announced that he was a candidate, the headline in the *Atlanta Constitution* read JIMMY WHO IS RUNNING FOR WHAT!?

When he left the governor's mansion in 1975, Carter began devoting his full energy to winning the Democratic presidential nomination. That year he was on the campaign trail outside Georgia for about 250 days, to little effect. In October of that year pollsters asked the public to rank the possible contenders for the Democratic nomination. Carter's name did not even come up.

But Carter was just getting started, working on a plan of action with Hamilton Jordan, Jody Powell, and other smart young Georgian hotshots who were beginning to sign on to manage his campaign. "Our strategy," he recalled, "was simple: Make a total effort all over the nation."

This was nowhere near as glamorous as it may have sounded. The real effort would have to begin in Iowa, which was where the campaign officially began. The Iowa caucuses are a complex system in which that state holds meetings to decide who it will nominate. Iowa is the first state in the union to make its decision. Carter realized that Iowa would be supremely important if he was going to generate any attention and momentum.

"Those were the lonely days," Carter recalled later. "Often just Jody and I would fly into the state in a small private plane. When I began my campaign I didn't have a built-in organization. There were no television cameras, no tape recorders, no radio reporters. I was a lonely unknown candidate. I came here looking for a TV camera; I never found it. I never saw a tape recorder or a radio reporter. But I found a lot of people who were interested in me. And we began going from one living room to another, from one labor hall to another, from one livestock feed hall to another. I would make a ten-minute speech and then answer questions for forty-five minutes, and that personal give-and-take was the decisive factor in getting me known."

Carter's famous attention to detail was crucial in this phase of the campaign. No one who gave a donation, or for that matter expressed any kind of an interest at all, was allowed to slip through the net. Their names were gathered and they were asked for further support. Often Carter wrote personal, handwritten notes to people who had been helpful.

In the end, when the dust cleared, the governor nobody knew had won the Iowa caucuses. "Anyone could have done it," a woman involved in political life in Iowa told reporter Kandy Stroud. "The trouble is, no one else worked as hard."

The sentiment was echoed by another supporter, who told Stroud, "Iowa was no phenomenon. There was nothing but hard work, organization, and leadership.

Jimmy Carter outworked everyone. He's tireless."

The campaign, now in the national spotlight, continued its inexhaustable roll. Next came the primaries in New Hampshire, where Carter faced ten other men, most of them better-known than he, who were jostling to get to the front of the Democrat pack and win the nomination. Astoundingly Carter won New Hampshire decisively as well.

Meanwhile the Republicans were deciding who their candidate would be in the general election in November. President Ford, who had been chosen by President Nixon to take his place following Nixon's resignation, was hoping to serve another term. However Ford was fighting off a strong challenge from the governor of California, Ronald Reagan. While Reagan, a former movie star, came off as suave and polished, Ford had an unfortunate tendency to trip and fall exactly when the news cameras were running, including a particularly bad moment when he stumbled down the stairs of the presidential airplane, *Air Force One*. He also frequently misspoke, saying things he may or may not have realized were mistakes. It became a sort of sport among reporters to follow his falls and errors. In a line that stuck to Ford like glue, someone dredged up a joke that the late president Lyndon Johnson had made about him years before: "He can't walk and chew gum at the same time."

Nonetheless as the primaries unfolded in state after state, Ford was able to hold on to his lead. Meanwhile Carter was campaigning like mad, moving ahead of his rivals, one of whom was Governor George Wallace, the segregationist from Alabama. Carter and his wife crisscrossed the country, traveling more than five hundred thousand miles in the course of the campaign.

Rosalynn was by no means an unwilling partner in this grueling endeavor. "She's one tough lady," Carter aide Hamilton Jordan said. "It's hard to imagine, but if one person wants him to be president more than Jimmy, it's Rosalynn." When her husband was governor, Rosalynn had been dubbed the Steel Magnolia by political pundits. Though she was small and soft-voiced, she was unstoppable when she had a goal. Once, during those years, she was supposed to give a speech, but accidentally got locked into a stall in the ladies' room.

Not wanting to mess up her suit and corsage by wiggling under the door, she simply climbed onto the toilet seat and hoisted herself over. Then she gave her speech. And during the presidential campaign, when she and her husband were in St. Augustine, Florida, the night before that state's primary, the mayor chose not to attend Carter's rally. So she went to the building where he was holding a town meeting and silently confronted him. There was nothing he could do but introduce her and welcome her. She shook hands with people and left.

Her press secretary told Kandy Stroud that Rosalynn is a woman who never missed an opportunity to learn, to grow, to stretch herself. "She gets better at what she does and more sure of herself all the time," she said. "The campaign is an incredible story of how two people just got in a car and drove from town to town and got in the newspapers and got on radio and TV. Her whole life has just been growing to this point."

By summertime Carter had rolled right over the opposition. On July 14, 1976, at the Democratic convention at Madison Square Garden in New York City, he was nominated by a cheering, jubilant crowd.

He was the candidate the Democrats had chosen to face Gerald Ford that November.

Carter chose as his running mate a senator from Minnesota named Walter Mondale. It made sense to choose someone from the North to attract those voters who were not sure about a candidate from the Deep South. (There had not been a president from that region of the country since Zachary Taylor in 1849.) The choice would also help with the labor unions who might have been uncomfortable with Carter the Southerner; the big unions have always been important to the Democrats, and the South has been traditionally antiunion.

Now that there were just two candidates, the campaign was off and running for real. At the beginning Carter had a large, comfortable lead over Gerald Ford. The economy was not in good shape, and about eight percent of American workers were unemployed, a number that was painfully high. Inflation was running high too, meaning that it took more and more money to buy less. People were miserable and worried about the future. Ford's response was to have buttons made up that read WIN, short for "Whip Inflation Now." It did

Jimmy Carter
and his sister
Gloria
(Georgia,
ca. 1928).

Jimmy Carter, as a boy, petting a
colt in a field (Georgia, ca. 1920).

Jimmy Carter in his Naval
Academy uniform (ca. 1946).

Presidential and vice presidential candidates Jimmy Carter and Walter Mondale stand with their wives at a 1976 Democratic Convention press conference (New York City, 1976).

Chief Justice Warren Burger administers the oath of office to Jimmy Carter as the United States' 39th president on January 20, 1977.

President Jimmy Carter
in his White House office
(1979).

President Jimmy Carter crouches in his peanut patch on the Carter farm
while brother, Billy, looks on (Plains, Georgia, 1977).

Panama's military leader General Omar Torrijos Herrera embraces President Jimmy Carter after the two leaders signed the ratified Panama Canal Treaties (Panama City, Panama 1977).

Egyptian president Anwar Sadat, U.S. president Jimmy Carter, and Israeli prime minister Menachem Begin sign the peace treaty between Israel and Egypt in the White House (September 17, 1978).

President Jimmy Carter hugs his mother, Lillian, (Washington, D.C., ca. 1977-1980).

Egyptian president Anwar Sadat and his wife, Jehan, pose with President Jimmy Carter and First Lady Rosalynn Carter at the pyramids in Giza, Egypt (March 10, 1979).

Former President Jimmy Carter, leading an international team of observers monitoring the election process, greets Haitian presidential candidate, Father Jean-Bertrand Aristide, on the eve of the Haitian presidential elections (Port-au-Prince, Haiti, December 15, 1990).

(Left to right) Former presidents George Bush, Ronald Reagan, Jimmy Carter, Gerald Ford, and Richard Nixon gather for the dedication of the Ronald Reagan Presidential Library (Ventura, California, ca. 1991).

Former President Jimmy Carter reads *The Little Baby Snoogle-Fleejer* with his daughter, Amy. He wrote the book, and his daughter did the illustrations (ca. 1995).

Former President Jimmy Carter with Palestinian leader Yasser Arafat.
Carter went to Gaza as an international election observer (Gaza,
Palestine, January 21, 1996).

Former President Jimmy
Carter participates in the
Jimmy Carter Work Project,
which is a Habitat for
Humanity annual event to
build homes for the poor
(South Korea, August
2001).

Former President Jimmy Carter made a bold push for democracy in communist Cuba. While in Havana, Carter threw the first pitch in a baseball game beside Cuban president Fidel Castro (May 2002).

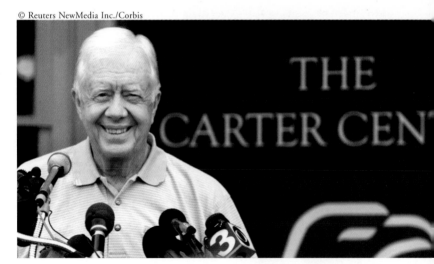

Former President Jimmy Carter addresses a crowd in Plains, Georgia, after he was awarded the Nobel Peace Prize (October 11, 2002).

not catch on, to say the least. In fact it became a laughingstock. The other thing that held Ford back was his association with his former boss, Richard Nixon. Try as Ford might to distance himself from Nixon, Carter always managed to bring the subject back to the disgraced president and his pardon by Ford. The country was trying hard to forget the scandal and misery that the Vietnam War and Watergate had brought and move on. Carter, the fresh face from the Georgia peanut fields, was looking better and better.

Peanuts, in fact, were everywhere in Carter's campaign. His plane was called *Peanut One*. The legions of hopeful young people who tramped from door to door all over the country campaigning for him were called the Peanut Brigade. And at Carter's campaign stops there were frequent appearances of "Mr. Peanut," a large walking legume made of foam and wire.

But then Carter made a serious miscalculation. He decided to grant an interview to *Playboy* magazine. The interviewer was a respected and serious writer, but the fact that the piece was in a magazine filled with naked women struck people as unseemly, to say the least. This was compounded by the fact that the interview was wide-ranging and personal, and Carter ended up saying some extremely private things that would cause him no end of trouble. "I've looked on a lot of women with lust," he admitted. "I've committed adultery in my heart many times. This is something that God recognizes I will do . . . and God forgives me for it." Although these revelations were hardly startling for a red-blooded American man—after all, he hadn't actually *done* anything—the nation found the statements uncomfortable, embarrassing, and just plain silly. Now it was Carter's turn to become a laughing-stock to a press eager for any juicy material that parted from politics-as-usual. Poor Rosalynn was put in the uncomfortable position of having to fend off some very personal questions in the weeks following the article's appearance.

Next came a series of debates. Neither candidate did particularly well. Ford's worst moment was when he insisted that Eastern Europe was not under Soviet domination, which any fifth-grader at the time would probably have known was untrue. Nonetheless he stuck to his guns in the following days, only making things worse. Carter, on the other hand, had lost all his natural bounce in front of the camera and looked wooden and boring.

By Election Day the great enthusiasm for the newcomer from Plains had become greatly diluted, and the polls were now showing the candidates in a dead heat.

The Carters flew back to Plains to cast their votes on the big day. They showed up at the polls at seven thirty in the morning. And then they waited. It was a long, tense day that ended after three o'clock the following morning when Mississippi voted for Carter. He had won.

When all the ballots were counted, Jimmy Carter had squeaked by with a very tight victory. He had won 49.9 percent of the popular votes, and 297 electoral votes. Ford had gotten 47.9 percent of the popular vote and 240 electoral votes. It was hardly a landslide for Carter, and it meant that he was not destined to take over the Oval Office with the enthusiastic support that every new president hopes for. The closeness of the vote meant it would be much harder for Carter to govern.

CHAPTER 6

PRESIDENT CARTER

Jimmy Carter was determined that his presidency would be different from the ones that had preceded it. There had been much talk of the "imperial presidencies" of Richard Nixon and Lyndon Johnson before him, presidencies in which power had been abused and things had been done in secret. Carter was going to wash all that away.

And so on Inauguration Day, January 20, 1977, he leaned forward in the limousine as it slowly moved from the U.S. Capitol, where he had just been sworn in, toward the White House. He tapped the Secret Service driver on the shoulder and asked him to stop the car. Then he touched Rosalynn's hand. "Let's go," he said. They got out of the car and began to walk toward the White House.

At first the crowd was stunned and thought something was wrong with the car. Then the Carters' three sons and their wives fell in with them, along with nine-year-old Amy. "It seemed that a shock wave went through the crowd," Carter wrote later in his presidential memoir, *Keeping Faith*. "There were gasps of astonishment and cries of 'They're walking! They're walking!' The excitement flooded over us; we responded to the people with broad smiles and proud steps. It was bitterly cold, but we felt warm inside."

Thus began the nonimperial presidency. Carter could not have chosen a better way to signal to America that things were about to be different. Pomp and circumstance were for others; he was not interested. There were other changes too. He put a stop to the endless playing of "Hail to the Chief" every time he walked into an official gathering. He sold off the presidential yacht. Rosalynn never got around to ordering new White House china, something that is traditional for First Ladies to do. They immediately made the decision to send Amy to public school in Washington, D.C.—a choice that was unheard-of. And when Carter went on television to talk to the American people in a fireside chat about energy conservation, he wore a comfortable cardigan, giving the impression of informality as well as reminding viewers to turn down their thermostats and save energy.

America was wildly happy about this new, no-frills president. Perhaps things would be different this time. Carter was a deeply moral man, a president who spoke about self-determination for all countries and human rights for all people. He appointed more women and African Americans to his government than any president before him. In the spirit of the forgiveness in which he so deeply believed, Carter's first official act was to pardon those who had fled the country to avoid being drafted during the Vietnam War. Perhaps, everyone thought, this country would return to the values upon which it had been built, and life would get better for everyone.

Of course there was no way this elation could last. Problems and conflicts were bound to come up, and they were only worsened by Carter's personality. The same character traits that had catapulted him from Plains to the White House now started to work against him.

As more and more people got to know Jimmy Carter, they found that they weren't really getting to know him at all. He seemed to be a man of a thousand contradictions. He could be tremendously warm—and also ice-cold. Sometimes he was very thoughtful, sometimes casually hurtful. His famous attention to detail now became known as micromanaging, getting caught up in details that should have been handled by those serving under him.

And, most bewilderingly, the man who had placed so much emphasis on an open presidency was closed to almost everyone around him. "Getting to know Jimmy Carter was one of the most baffling experiences of my life," says political writer Kandy Stroud. "Even intimate staff members have been known to say the process of understanding Jimmy Carter is mystifying. One of them said, 'To know Jimmy Carter for six days is to love him; to work for him for six weeks is to detest him, and after six months you begin to respect him.'" He did not appear to have much of a sense of humor. Reporters and fellow politicians alike found him fascinating and respected his great intelligence, but not many genuinely liked him.

Carter quickly began to be seen as cold, arrogant, and unable to compromise with others. On occasion he insulted or ignored people in Congress—even those in his own party—and they repaid him by knocking down some of the first legislation he proposed on consumer protection. He did accomplish a great deal in the four years he was president, but it was seldom without congressional interference. At one point Congress reworked Carter's tax-reform plan to ensure big tax breaks for people or groups who had contributed money to its members. In response, the president called them "a pack of ravenous wolves."

Two of Carter's main concerns were the problems of energy and peace in the Middle East. There was an ongoing, serious shortage of energy supply in this country, and Carter was committed to dealing with it. The United States was more and more dependent on the oil-producing Arab nations, gobbling up a quarter of the region's entire world supply. Americans used almost three times the amount of energy per person as people in other countries did. (Unfortunately these statistics have remained constant into the twenty-first century.)

The winter in which Carter took office was one of the coldest on record. Soon after the election Carter introduced an Emergency Natural Gas Act, which allowed the federal government to distribute natural gas supplies to the states that needed them most. In August the president also created a brand-new Department of Energy to demonstrate how serious he was about solving the problem. Being a nuclear engineer Carter understood technical energy issues very well, especially the difficulties of nuclear power plants. He got Congress to shut down a large reactor because its design would increase the risk of deadly plutonium getting into the wrong hands later on.

In the area of foreign policy Carter wanted to help to bring about a solution to the seemingly endless cycle of war and bitterness that had existed in the Middle East since Israel became a nation in 1948. He quickly began working with the leaders of Israel and Egypt, meeting with newly elected Prime Minister Menachem Begin of Israel in July, and contacting President Anwar Sadat of Egypt by letter to ask for his support in the peace effort.

In a controversial move that was to have long-lasting effects, Carter pushed through the establishment of formal diplomatic relations with Communist China. Doing so meant that relations would have to be severed with the island of Taiwan. A democratic republic that had broken off from the mainland in 1949, Taiwan is still claimed by Mainland China. Carter's action was hotly opposed by conservatives in the legislature, but it gradually served to open Communist China's markets and government to Western influences, and led to that country's being one of the United States' major trading partners.

Carter's first really big dispute with Congress was over the Panama Canal. The canal has always been of critical importance to this country's economy, being the only way that ships could travel between the Atlantic and Pacific Oceans without having to sail all the way down around the southernmost tip of South America. In 1903 a treaty had been hastily drawn up between the United States and the Republic of Panama. Acting for Panama, Carter explains in *Keeping Faith*, was a French businessman who had not been to Panama in eighteen years and probably did not even have the authority to negotiate it. The terms of the treaty were extremely favorable to the United States. The United States had been allowed total authority over the land surrounding the narrow canal, while Panama had none—a fact the Panamanians bitterly resented.

Under agreements that had been half-heartedly negotiated, the canal was to revert to Panamanian control at some point. Carter believed, as a moral issue, that he should negotiate the return of the canal to the Panamanians. But there were many conservatives in Congress who believed we should not give it back since a lot of U.S. money had gone into building it in the first place. Carter was charged with negotiating the details of the handover, including the question of whether the United States could defend the Canal Zone from any attack, even if the United States was no longer in control of it. Carter negotiated an agreement with Panama that said Panama would have full control of the canal back by 1999. But he did not include members of Congress in the talks and kept them poorly informed about what he was doing. They were angry, and they fought back. They only passed the agreement after a side deal had been worked out between one of the senators and the Panamanian president, insuring that the United States could intervene to protect the canal. In the end

Carter got his treaty passed—but not before Congress had embarrassed him.

There were some personal problems that bedeviled Carter's presidency as well. In the summer of 1977 Bert Lance, his budget director and close friend, was accused of financial misdeeds when he'd been a banker back in Georgia. The heat became more and more intense, and Lance finally had to resign—though Carter stuck by him. Lance was eventually cleared of all charges, but not before serious damage had been done to Carter, who until then had been perceived by the public as squeaky-clean. He was tarnished by the affair and could not shake the taint of home-state corruption.

In addition the president had a problem with his brother, Billy. Billy was mostly an embarrassment, doing such things as joining a business venture to produce Billy Beer and posing for photos with cans of it. But in 1980 there was a more serious problem. Billy was found to have accepted a quarter of a million dollars from the government of Libya, which was run by a military strongman and—despite the United States having diplomatic relations with the country—had been considered a terrorist nation for years. Most likely it was simply an error in judgment about a business deal involving the importing of Libyan oil. But, naturally, the affair reflected badly on Billy's brother, the president.

In December of 1979 the Soviet Union invaded Afghanistan, which is of vital strategic importance in the region's oil production and transportation. The United States was furious and began providing training and weaponry to the mujahideen, the Islamic guerrilla fighters who were resisting the Soviet troops. (It was this same training and weaponry that was eventually turned against the United States when it invaded Afghanistan in the aftermath of September 11, 2001.) Carter was so incensed at the Soviet invasion that he decided the United States would boycott the 1980 Summer Olympic Games in Moscow. The decision proved to be very unpopular. The war in Afghanistan was far away, and Americans did not understand why the young athletes who had worked so hard to get to the Olympics should be punished for a conflict that seemingly had nothing to do with our country.

The Soviet invasion also put a dent in crucially

important arms-control talks Carter was having with that country. The United States and the Soviet Union had already signed a treaty to reduce the number of nuclear missiles both countries had, but the Senate would not ratify it following the invasion of Afghanistan. Carter withdrew the treaty, but both countries agreed to abide by its terms.

Energy was also the source of a good deal of trouble in Carter's life as president. The issue was something he worked very hard on throughout his term of office, and he affected many changes that ended up having positive effects for many years to come. He pushed through legislation that would increase U.S. stockpiles of oil, which meant that prices at American gas pumps would drop considerably in the 1980s. He increased funding for research on alternative sources of power, such as solar and wind, although Congress defeated a measure Carter had proposed that would have helped energy researchers. But energy policy was technical and not easily understood by the average citizen—meaning that Carter got little credit for his efforts.

And meanwhile something happened that seriously

dragged Carter's popularity down. The oil-producing nations decided to get together and form the Organization of Petroleum Exporting Countries (OPEC) that would make policy and set prices for all of them as a group. OPEC decided to cut production and raise the price of oil. Suddenly there were gas shortages and skyrocketing prices at the pump. During Carter's term the price of a barrel of crude oil went from thirteen dollars to thirty-four dollars.

Because of the shortage, cars had to line up, sometimes for hours, to fill up at beleaguered gas stations. Because it cost so much more for the fuel that such industries as trucking and aviation needed to move people and goods, inflation spiraled upward. Prices for everything got higher. And, to make things a little worse, on March 28, 1979, there was an accident at the Three Mile Island nuclear reactor near Harrisburg, Pennsylvania. The worst accident in the history of American nuclear power, it resulted in the partial meltdown of one of the plant's reactor cores. For a few tense and terrifying days until the damage was contained, it seemed possible that the entire East Coast would be engulfed by deadly radioactivity.

Everyone blamed Carter for the energy crisis. Carter, meanwhile, did not have the communication skills to defuse the nation's anger. "He seemed aloof and condescending, stiff and impersonal with reporters," according to PBS's www.theamericanpresident.org. "They chafed at his moralistic, 'eat your peas' attitudes, and portrayed him as either a cynical and manipulative politician or an amateurish incompetent. . . . His media images always came out wrong."

In an attempt to give his image a fresh start, Carter asked for and received the resignations of a large number of people in his administration. His idea was that it would look as if he was firmly taking the reins of his presidency and changing things for the better. Instead it was interpreted as a sign that things had spun out of control. And in some countries with different forms of government, it was mistakenly believed that the changes meant the United States government had fallen.

Carter, it seemed, could do no right when it came to his public image.

CHAPTER 7

CLIFFHANGER AT CAMP DAVID

Through all this Carter never stopped speaking out about his greatest personal causes: peace and human rights throughout the world. Behind the scenes he kept plugging away at what was to be his greatest triumph as president: a peace agreement between Egypt and Israel. In September of 1978 he convinced President Sadat and Prime Minister Begin to come to the United States and try, face-to-face, to work out some sort of agreement with Carter's help. Carter thought they should hold the meetings at Camp David, the country retreat in Maryland that presidents use to relax, hold meetings, and think.

About an hour from Washington, in the magnificent Blue Ridge Mountains, Camp David was built by President Franklin Roosevelt in 1942. It was originally called Shangri-La, after a mythical Himalayan paradise in a popular book of the 1930s, but it was later renamed by President Dwight Eisenhower after his grandson, David. Camp David has served as the peaceful backdrop for a number of important conferences between U.S. presidents and foreign heads of state, starting with a meeting during World War II between President Roosevelt and British prime minister Winston Churchill. Camp David's lovely two-thousand-acre grounds, which include a swimming pool, movie theater, walking paths, and separate cabins for visiting dignitaries, are surrounded by maximum-security fencing and armed guards to protect the heads of state within.

It was here, Carter felt, that intensive talks between the leaders would have the best chance of succeeding. To try to foster as friendly and informal an atmosphere as possible, he invited all three wives to attend as well, although as it turned out, Mrs. Sadat had to stay in Paris with a sick grandchild. "There was no compatibility at all between Begin and Sadat on which to base any progress," Carter wrote later. "This warmer relationship would have to be created from scratch." In setting up this conference, in trying to mediate a difficult dispute between two other countries, Carter was attempting to accomplish something that no American president had done since Theodore Roosevelt had helped the Russians and the Japanese negotiate an end to their war in 1905.

Each of the three leaders brought a small team of eminent political leaders from his own country to help in the negotiations. There were many complicated points to be worked out and no history of goodwill between the two Middle Eastern nations. War after war had taken many lives from each, and Israel's neighbors did not even recognize its right to exist. Carter was there to try to facilitate the discussions, suggest compromise solutions, and offer financial or security aid from the United States where it could be helpful. True to his careful, detail-oriented nature, President Carter took meticulous notes throughout the process. In this aspect of character he was closer to Menachem Begin, although he felt a much warmer bond in general with Anwar Sadat.

The negotiations were rocky. At times it seemed as

if the two sides were getting close to an agreement, and then suddenly negotiations would fall apart and they would have to start over. Each leader would have to go back to his own government and people and try to sell the compromises he would inevitably have to make, and all three knew it would not be easy. Each leader was highly intelligent, and each had brought smart advisers with him. The issues were a source of great bitterness. What would happen to the city of Jerusalem, holy to three religions and fought over since the establishment of the State of Israel? What would happen to the Sinai Peninsula, desert land Israel had seized in a war started by its neighbors in 1967? What would be the fate of the Jewish settlers who had built homes on other land won in that war? What would become of the Palestinians, who had been living in Israel before it became a nation and were now stateless? On and on it wore, day after day, back and forth.

"Every time they got in the same room," Carter told an interviewer later, "we went backward instead of forward. So Begin and Sadat stayed separate. And I would go to one, then go to the other one, back and forth." The two leaders, he said, did not actually see each other for the last ten days of the conference.

And then on the eleventh day catastrophe struck. Carter received a phone call: Just as the gap between the countries' positions had finely narrowed, negotiations had broken down utterly. Sadat had packed his bags and asked for a helicopter to take him to the airport. It was over. Carter had known since the previous day that the two nations had stopped negotiating and was already talking with his own advisers about how to break the bad news to the American public that the whole effort had been a failure. But he had not expected this; he was at least expecting a civilized ending to the conference, with the dignitaries departing on some sort of hopeful note for the future. This finale was awful, and its consequences for the worldwide political situation would be dire.

Carter asked all his aides to leave him for a little while. "I remained alone in the little study where most of the negotiations had taken place," he writes. "I moved over to the window and looked out to the Catoctin Mountains and prayed fervently for a few minutes that somehow we could find peace."

Then, on an impulse, he got dressed in formal clothes and went over to Sadat's cabin. Sadat was on the front porch with his advisers, waiting to leave.

Carter walked into the cabin with Sadat and said what was in his heart. "I explained to him," he writes, "the extremely serious consequences of his unilaterally breaking off the negotiations: that his action would harm the relationship between Egypt and the United States, he would be violating his personal promise to me, and the onus for failure would be on him . . . I told him it would damage one of my most precious possessions—his friendship and our mutual trust."

Sadat was firm, but Carter persisted, telling Sadat that he simply had to keep working at it with him for another day or two. The main problem, it emerged, was that one of Begin's advisers, a respected Israeli war hero, had told Sadat that Israel would not sign any agreements. Sadat felt that his time was being wasted and that Israel was simply there to find out what Egypt was willing to give up in future negotiations.

This was a serious problem, and Carter had to

think fast to deal with it. He made Sadat a promise to ensure that his position would be protected: Carter would guarantee that if any country rejected *any* part of the agreements, not one part would remain in effect.

That promise was enough to get Sadat to reconsider and stay on. Carter was very grateful. He decided to visit Sadat in his cabin that night with the vice president and secretary of state. It was purely a social call, to show how much they appreciated his staying. They all watched Muhammad Ali win a boxing match, as Sadat was a big admirer of the fighter. Late that night Carter got the boxer on the phone, congratulated him, and invited his daughter to come and visit Amy at the White House. Ali was excited and pleased to get the call.

Work continued the next day with Carter going back and forth between the two sides, trying to stitch together an agreement that would hold. After one final breakthrough on the thirteenth day, Carter realized that he had gotten the Israeli group to agree to a set of terms that he knew Sadat would be willing to sign. He had his agreement.

Not surprisingly the agreement then proceeded to fall apart several more times. Each time the whole process seemed to have gone down the drain, Carter hammered away at both sides, coming up with new wording and approaches that would satisfy everyone.

And then finally there really was an agreement. All that remained was to get back to Washington and announce it to the public—and to keep Sadat and Begin away from each other until it was signed, just in case.

On September 17, 1978, at 10:15 in the evening, the Camp David Accords were signed. It was a moment of joy and triumph, and all three leaders, though dead tired, were flushed with the success they had achieved against all the odds. The agreement stipulated that Israel would pull out of the Sinai Peninsula, that Israel and Egypt would recognize each other's governments and establish normal diplomatic relations, and that Israel would promise to negotiate for peace with the Palestinians. The United States would establish military posts to guarantee that neither side would attack the other.

That year Begin and Sadat received the Nobel Peace Prize. When the Nobel Committee awarded the prize to Carter in 2002, they noted that Carter had not shared the 1978 award with those two leaders because nobody had thought to nominate him in time.

The Camp David Accords were only the beginning of the process, though. Carter has worked hard from that day forward to hang on to a shred of peace in the region, but it was not to be. The enmities are old and deep. Nothing is easy in the Middle East, and things quickly began to unravel. Before the year was out, Egypt was expelled from the Arab League, which was an organization of Arab countries.

Several years later on October 6, 1981, back home in Plains, Former President Jimmy Carter got a phone call soon after dawn. President Sadat, he was told, had survived an assassination attempt by religious extremists while reviewing a military parade in his country, and was only slightly wounded. Later that day the news changed. Anwar Sadat, Carter's good friend, was dead, murdered for the bravery he had shown in negotiating a peace agreement in a region that lived on war.

CHAPTER 8 ★

HOSTAGE IN THE WHITE HOUSE

Carter received a short-lived boost in his popularity after negotiating the treaty between Egypt and Israel but, true to the nature of his presidency, he was once again overwhelmed by circumstance—and this time he would not recover. This time the problem was Iran.

America's twentieth-century relationship with Iran had not been the finest chapter in its history. It was all about oil.

Large quantities of oil had been discovered in Iran, then known as Persia, in 1909. About three times the size of France, Iran became a hotly contested political pawn, first between the Germans, Russians, and the British in World War I, and later, during the long Cold War, between the Soviet Union and the West. Through the first half of the twentieth century, the British, through Shell Oil, which they owned with the Dutch, were able to buy as much oil as they wanted for next to nothing. But things changed in 1951 when a new prime minister in Iran, Mohammad Mosaddeq, decided that it was time for the foreign oil companies to go and kicked them out. This was not acceptable to the Western powers. They wanted to hang on to the oil and were afraid that the Soviet Union would take over Iran and turn it Communist. So the U.S. Central Intelligence Agency (CIA) acted, staging a coup that removed Mosaddeq. In his place they installed Mohammad Reza Pahlavi, known as the Shah, or "king." He came from a family that had originally seized power in Iran in 1925. A condition of the Shah's taking the throne was that he would turn over eighty percent of Iran's oil production to British and American oil companies.

The Shah began an ambitious program of modernizing his country. He started a program to redistribute huge amounts of land, taking it out of the hands of a few wealthy landowners and giving it to the farmers who worked it. He fought to raise the level of literacy, as well as to improve the status of women. For these things and others, he was heavily criticized by

Iranian Muslim leaders, and in 1964 he sent one of them, the Ayatollah Khomeini, into exile after one of the ayatollah's speeches sparked antigovernment riots.

But the Shah's regime became more and more repressive. His secret police, the Savak, spread terror through the country, abducting and torturing large numbers of people who were seen as enemies of the state. As hatred for the Shah began to mount so did the Iranians' animosity for the United States, which was understood to be keeping him in power.

Finally the dam broke. In 1979 there was a revolution in Iran. The Ayatollah Khomeini returned from exile in France to take control and set up a strictly religious Islamic government. Millions of Iranians poured into the streets chanting, "Death to America!"

The Shah was forced to flee. He went to Mexico, where he was diagnosed in October with cancer. Carter decided to let him come to New York for treatment.

On November 4, 1979, the situation exploded. Enraged that America was harboring the hated Shah, militant Muslim students, followers of the ayatollah, overran the U.S. Embassy in Tehran and took sixty-six

Americans hostage, calling them spies. They demanded that Carter turn over the Shah and force him to return the large sums of money that he had stashed outside of Iran. They wanted an apology from Carter.

Carter and his team tried to negotiate for the release of the hostages, but it was no use. On November 17 the Iranians did free thirteen of them. They were all women and African Americans, and their captors decided that they were not spies. Carter tried unsuccessfully to get other countries in the region to intercede on behalf of the hostages. At Carter's request even Pope John Paul II tried to talk Khomeini into releasing the hostages, but the ayatollah only made an insulting speech about the Catholic leader. There were still 570 Americans in Iran, and Carter, worried about their safety as well, ordered the companies who employed them to get them out of the country. The only thing Carter was sure of was that he would not turn the dying Shah over to the mobs in Iran.

Carter did what he could, which was not a great deal. No one was even sure if the hostages were still in the embassy. While his team studied the options for a military rescue, which were almost nonexistent, Carter met with the families of the hostages and shared his grief and fear with them. He had the State Department begin to deport Iranian students who were here illegally; many of the "students" had not actually been in any school for years. He froze all monies that the Iranian government had in U.S. bank accounts. He prohibited the sale of Iranian oil to the United States.

But the hostage takers were heroes in their country, and in the face of Iran's hatred for America, which they called the great Satan, these measures had little or no effect. Oceans of people filled the streets of Tehran day after day, burning American flags and chanting slogans. It was a standoff. The clock ticked, the days went by, the weeks ground on. The Shah, recognizing the problems he was causing for his hosts in the United States, offered to go back to Mexico. Carter hoped this would ease tension with Iran. But Mexico, which had agreed to accept the exiled leader, suddenly changed its mind, dashing Carter's hopes.

Meanwhile Americans were growing restless and impatient. Taking a cue from a 1973 song, Americans began to tie yellow ribbons everywhere, signifying they would welcome the hostages home, ushering in the American tradition of ribbon wearing. A new late-night news program, *Nightline*, ran daily updates that marked off each additional day: "America Held Hostage—Day 67." This only reinforced the growing feeling that Carter was weak and ineffectual.

But life still had to go on, and it was time for a new political season to begin. The president announced his candidacy for reelection on December 4. On December 27 the Soviets invaded Afghanistan. It was not a good time for the Carter presidency.

Carter knew he was very vulnerable to a defeat, and his staff knew it too. He brought them together and told them that anyone who wanted to get off the boat was welcome to do so. Nobody did—at least not then.

It was clear that Senator Edward Kennedy, known as Ted, was thinking about running against Carter for the nomination. Kennedy was a formidable opponent. As the younger brother of the slain President John Kennedy and Attorney General Robert Kennedy, he was a member of the Democrats' first family. He had also been a very influential senator himself for many years, committed to liberal ideals, and had run for president before. To make things worse, Carter had to leave the campaigning to his wife and the vice president, so that he could stay in the White House and concentrate on the hostage crisis.

And then, in April of 1980, disaster came on top of catastrophe. In absolute secrecy, Carter had authorized a daring military mission to rescue the hostages in Iran. There were enormous distances to be covered between any possible starting point and Tehran. The rescue helicopters were to take off on April 24 from a remote spot in the Iranian desert called Desert One. They would fly into Tehran, swiftly extract the prisoners, and fly out.

At about three fifteen in the afternoon Carter and his advisers started hearing about problems with the mission. A busload of people had seen the helicopters and would have to be whisked away to Egypt so they could not alert anyone to the U.S. military presence in Iran. But everything still looked positive. Then a sandstorm came up. Three of the helicopters developed mechanical problems, and the entire mission was aborted. But it was now too late. Suddenly there were reports that one of the other helicopters was missing, and nobody knew its whereabouts. And at 5:58 P.M., the really bad news came: In the swirling dust of the sandstorm, the missing helicopter had smashed into a transport plane on the ground. Both aircraft had burst into flames, and eight soldiers were killed. It was, Carter wrote, one of the worst days of his life.

"The cancellation of the mission," he sadly wrote in his diary that night, "was caused by a strange series of mishaps—almost completely unpredictable. The operation itself was well planned. The men were well trained. We had every possibility of success. . . ."

If there was an absolute low point to the Carter presidency, this was probably it. The disastrous mission could not have been a worse piece of luck. Carter, stricken with grief for the men who had died, had to tell the public what had happened. His secretary of state, Cyrus Vance, had been so opposed to the mission because of the danger to the hostages that he had quietly resigned before the mission was launched. Now this, too, had to become public knowledge. Though, as Carter writes, he was grateful for the fact that the American people were supportive, the incident could not help but ultimately become another nail in his political coffin. It was easy for opponents to subtly paint him as weak and incompetent.

Ted Kennedy, meanwhile, was moving across the country like a steamroller. He won primaries in a number of large, key states, like California, New York, Pennsylvania, and Michigan. That July, Carter's approval rating was the lowest ever measured by opinion polls in modern times.

By August, however, Carter had won a substantial number of delegates in other states. At the Democratic convention Kennedy decided to withdraw from the race, while making sure that some of the policies he believed in would be included in the Democrats' program. Carter was nominated to be the Democratic candidate in the November general election.

Meanwhile California governor Ronald Reagan had coasted easily to the front of the Republican pack. Now he was the man Carter would have to beat in November.

Reagan, having been an actor for many years, was comfortable in front of television cameras and had an instinctive understanding of how to talk to the American people. While Carter, in a speech, had given his countrymen the gloomy news that there was a "malaise," or sickness, affecting the nation, Reagan told them that everything was going to be just fine if they stuck with him. His campaign slogan said that it was "morning in America." While Carter looked stiff and wooden during their televised debates, Reagan was polished and relaxed.

Behind the scenes Carter continued to negotiate for the release of the hostages. He got to know their courageous but desperate families. He read their letters. He felt he knew each one personally.

There were changes going on in Iran as well. The country was in the process of organizing its new government, and not without bloodshed. In the wake of the rescue attempt decisions were also being made about the hostages, who were separated and moved to secret locations; Carter learned much later from them that the rescue mission did seem to scare their captors into treating them better.

As the country realized that the hostages were not coming home anytime soon, Carter's approval ratings in the polls plummeted with stomach-dropping speed. When Election Day arrived on November 4, 1980, the president still had not been able to make a deal with the Iranians for the release of the hostages. Time had run out.

When all the votes were counted that night, the numbers were beyond terrible. Carter got about thirty-five million votes to Reagan's forty-four million. But the really bad news was in the electoral votes. Because the electoral votes of any state go to the candidate who has won the majority of the popular vote and Reagan carried forty-four states, he won a whopping 489 electoral votes. Carter's six-state win earned just forty-nine electoral votes. It was a landslide for Ronald Reagan. The country wanted a change.

However, Carter would be president until Inauguration Day, January 20, 1981, and there was still a great deal he could do. During this period, he pushed through some of the most important environmental legislation the United States has ever seen. He created a huge wildlife preserve in Alaska, doubling the size of the United States' protected wilderness. And he also approved creation of the Superfund, which put aside money to clean up the most polluted toxic waste sites in the country.

Naturally Carter desperately wanted the hostages to be released before he left office, so he stepped up his efforts to convince the Iranians to let them go. Back in October the Iranians, communicating through Germany, had let it be known that they might be willing to negotiate a deal. They wanted the huge amount of their country's money—some twelve billion dollars—that had been frozen in U.S. bank accounts to be returned. They wanted the Shah's money, which they did not know had been largely moved out of the United States by his family. (At great risk to himself, Sadat had offered asylum in Egypt to the Shah, who eventually died there in July.) The Iranians also wanted a promise that the United States would stay out of their affairs, which Carter was happy to give. Meanwhile the situation had become more precarious for the hostages because Iran's neighbor Iraq had invaded it.

The negotiations continued after the election and right through January until at last the two sides were in agreement. The amount of money that would actually be released had been whittled down to some three billion dollars. Now, as the chapter drew to a close, the hard part was logistics—getting all the U.S. banks and financial institutions that had been holding the money to transfer it at the same time. Some of them balked; some had trouble with the complicated financial arrangements. The night before Reagan's inauguration, Carter and his team stayed up all night trying to make it happen. Every time things seemed to be going smoothly, there would be some snag with the electronic funds transfers.

Finally it was time to leave. At 11 A.M., the Reagans arrived at the White House to pick up the Carters and go to the noon inauguration on the steps of the Capitol. Time had run out.

At 12:33 P.M. on Tuesday, January 20, 1981, Carter got the call from the Secret Service. The hostages, after 444 days in captivity, had been released. Their plane had taken off and they were on their way home.

Jimmy Carter was no longer president.

★ ★ ★

The first visitor he'd had when he had taken office, Carter tells us in *Keeping Faith*, was Max Cleland. Cleland was a young man from Georgia whom Carter had appointed his Administrator of Veterans Affairs. (In 1997 he went on to become U.S. senator from Georgia.) Cleland had served in the Vietnam War, where a grenade had exploded near him. He had lost both legs and his right arm.

Cleland was also Carter's last official visitor to the Oval Office on January 20, 1981. He came to say goodbye, and he carried with him a plaque. On it was a quote from Thomas Jefferson:

I HAVE THE CONSOLATION TO REFLECT THAT DURING THE PERIOD OF MY ADMINISTRATION NOT A DROP OF THE BLOOD OF A SINGLE CITIZEN WAS SHED BY THE SWORD OF WAR.

"This is something I will always cherish," Carter wrote in his diary that day.

CHAPTER 9

WAGING PEACE

The biggest disappointment to the Carters was that so much work remained to be done, and they were no longer in a position to do it. Rosalynn felt the pain of this very keenly. "It didn't seem fair," she said, "that everything we had hoped for, all our plans and dreams for the country could have been gone when the votes were counted on Election Day." Amy, meanwhile, was brokenhearted to have to say good-bye to her school friends.

After the initial shock of their shattering defeat began to wear off, the Carters started to take stock of their lives. Now guarded, as are all former presidents, by Secret Service officers, the family went home to their old house in Plains. They visited with neighbors, went fishing, traveled, talked, and read. They realized that they had left the White House with personal debt from the presidential campaigns and would have to slowly pay it off. They decided to sell off the peanut warehouse, as they were not much interested in going back to their old life. Jimmy and Rosalynn knew they wanted to move forward, and gradually they began to do some serious thinking about the shape of their lives after the White House.

Carter was offered teaching posts at several universities, and even the presidencies of two of them. But he and Rosalynn wanted to do more. They wanted to keep working on the unfinished business of Carter's presidency, on the political and human issues that had so consumed them while he had been in office. Rosalynn had been with him every step of the way during those four years, discussing his decisions with him and offering him insight and support, and they wanted to continue in the same way, as a team. Gradually, when the cloud of political defeat lifted, they realized that part of what they felt was relief. They could continue their good work without the constant pressures of being in the public eye, without the polls, without the pundits on television. They were free, in a whole new way.

Jimmy Carter had never forgotten the lessons he'd learned from his mother, who had worked so hard all her life for the good of others. When she was in the Peace Corps at almost seventy years of age, she wrote these words from India to her daughter Gloria: "If I had one wish for my children, it would be that each of you would dare to do the things and reach for goals in your own lives that have meaning for you as individuals, doing as much as you can for everybody, but not worrying if you don't please everyone."

Guided as always by their Christian faith, the Carters began thinking about a center that would work in a serious way to address the problems of war, hunger, disease, and poverty. Gathering together a small group of experts, many of them from Carter's presidential administration, they began having meetings to talk about how best to accomplish this. They decided to team up with Emory University in Atlanta to make it happen. Their aim, they decided, was to create a center that did not just write position papers and have academic discussions. Their goal was action, not talk. What Carter wanted to do was not to take the place of the State Department or the United Nations, nor to interfere with their work, but to supplement their efforts. Carter knew that, with his special status as a private citizen who just happened to be an ex-president with personal ties to many world leaders, he could go into places and influence situations that the U.S. Government could not.

For the next few years, Jimmy and Rosalynn kept very busy. Jimmy worked on his memoir of the presidency, *Keeping Faith*, and went on tour to promote it. He traveled to the Middle East to foster peace there. But all the while, work was continuing on what would ultimately be the Carter Center. He and Rosalynn raised funds, found an unused piece of land in Atlanta to build on, and recruited distinguished scholars, diplomats, and scientists—including several Emory professors—who could be a part of the center's team. A great deal of work had already been done all over the world before the center actually opened its doors.

Finally the dream was real. The Carter Center opened officially on October 1, 1986.

In the years after the election Presidents Ronald

Reagan and Jimmy Carter had not had a very good relationship, by and large. Carter did not think much of Reagan's policies, and in fact, appearing on *60 Minutes*, had said that he "could not think of a single international or diplomatic achievement that's been realized by Ronald Reagan." Reagan had, for his part, snubbed and disparaged Carter in various ways. Their thinking about politics could not have been more opposite. And because Carter had been beaten so badly in the election, it was easy for Reagan and those in his administration to join in the general disrespect Carter was being afforded in the United States.

But at the opening of the Carter Center, Reagan gave a gracious and generous speech. "For myself," he said, "I can pay no higher honor than simply this: You gave of yourself to your country, gracing the White House with your passion and intellect and commitment."

When Carter stood to thank him, he said, grinning, "I think I understand more clearly than I ever had before why you won in November 1980, and I lost."

The Carter Center tore into its work from Day One. Together its members developed a statement of the five basic principles that would guide all its work in the future. They are posted on the Center's Web site:

1. The Center emphasizes action and results. Based on careful research and analysis, it is prepared to take timely action on important and pressing issues.

2. The Center does not duplicate the effective efforts of others.

3. The Center addresses difficult problems and recognizes the possibilities of failure as an acceptable risk.

4. The Center is nonpartisan and acts as a neutral in dispute resolution activities.

5. The Center believes that people can improve their lives when provided with the necessary skills, knowledge, and access to resources.

Public health around the world was one of the issues the Carters and their fellows plunged right into. "We believe good health is a basic human right," the former president has written, "especially among poor people afflicted with disease who are isolated, forgotten, ignored, and often without hope. Just to know that someone cares about them can not only ease their physical pain but also remove an element of alienation and anger that can lead to hatred and violence."

One of Jimmy Carter's first targets was the powerful tobacco industry, responsible for so many deaths and so much illness worldwide. For Carter the issue was personal. Both of his parents were heavy smokers, as was his sister Ruth. All three of them had died of pancreatic cancer (his brother, Billy, and sister Gloria would later succumb to the same disease), and after doing some research, Carter discovered that smokers had twice the risk of developing pancreatic cancer as did nonsmokers. Before the issue was popular, the Carter Center launched a campaign against smoking—starting with a ban on smoking at the center itself—one of the first to begin the national movement toward smoke-free workplaces. In one speech against smoking Carter made the potent point that more Colombians died from smoking cigarettes imported from the United States than Americans who died from using drugs smuggled to this country from Colombia.

Following in the footsteps of his mother, Carter began to use the center's resources to help eliminate such childhood diseases as measles, mumps, rubella, and polio—which, while almost nonexistent in the developed world, still killed and crippled millions of children in poorer countries, especially in Africa. Africa, in fact, became a major focus of the efforts of the center because its needs in every area of development were so desperate.

In large parts of Africa, as well as in other tropical areas, one of the major health problems was something called guinea worm disease, a horrible affliction that is transmitted through stagnant water.

The Carter Center, working with other organizations, began working on eradicating this horror in 1987. And now the center reports, "Guinea worm disease is set to become only the second disease to be wiped off the face of the earth. The numbers afflicted by this debilitating disease have been reduced worldwide by 98 percent, from 3.2 million cases in 1986 to less than 100,000 in 2001. Guinea worm will be the second disease to be eliminated from the world (after smallpox) and the first disease to be overcome without 'magic-bullet' vaccines and medications." Instead of treating the disease medically, the scourge has been destroyed by a patient program of spraying stagnant water and educating people to filter their drinking water and not to go in the water when they have blisters. The approach may not be as dramatic as magic bullets are, but it works.

Another of the center's causes is a different parasitic disease called river blindness, which is also prevalent in tropical areas. "Of the 18 million people infected with river blindness worldwide," says the Carter Center, "500,000 are blinded or visually impaired." In many villages near rivers in Africa, for example, most or all of the older people are blind and must be led around by the young. It is so common that there is a saying in West Africa: "Nearness to large rivers eats the eye."

Until 1987 there was no hope for people suffering from river blindness. But then something amazing happened. Scientists at Merck & Co., a large drug company, stumbled on the discovery that the heartworm medicine that had been developed for use in dogs would also kill the larvae that took over the bodies of river blindness victims. Just one pill a year would prevent or stop the progress of the disease. Merck decided it would distribute the drug for free in the stricken areas of the world until the disease was eradicated once and for all. But they needed a way to distribute the drug. They asked the Carter Center for help. "Let's do it," Carter said. The center coordinated its efforts and with other organizations', to both distribute the drug and to spray affected rivers with pesticides. Carter's connections with world leaders were essential in this effort. "What we can do at the Carter Center," he explained, "is go directly to the president of a nation, the prime minister of a nation, the health minister, the finance minister, the education minister, and the agricultural minister and get all of them working together. That's the only way to really reach every village." The project's target is to totally eliminate river blindness by the year 2007.

Meanwhile Carter did not stop his endless quest for peace in the world. He has become what history writer Douglas Brinkley termed a "tyrant for peace," traveling anywhere in the world he feels he might be able to help stop people from slaughtering each other. During his presidency and afterward, he has championed the cause of human rights all over Latin America, where dictators—many of whom had originally been nurtured by the United States— routinely suppressed dissent and tortured their own people. Jimmy and Rosalynn, through the center, have worked hard in country after country to restore peace, freedom, and democracy. Carter remains a beloved hero in much of Latin America, as he does in many other embattled parts of the world.

Carter and his wife have journeyed to Africa many times. In Ethiopia he helped to mediate a civil war that was destroying and starving the population. He went to the war-torn nation of Rwanda, where ancient tribal hatreds, newly stirred up, had set neighbor upon neighbor, killing almost a million people and making refugees of some two million more. Working with the leaders of several countries in the area, Carter helped negotiate peace and find ways to let the refugees go home safely. And in 1994 he went to North Korea to avert a dangerous crisis. That country, ruled by a Communist dictator and cut off for years from most of the world, was discovered to be developing nuclear weapons. President Clinton was faced with the decision of whether to invade the country to halt this dangerous proliferation. Carter, narrowly avoiding war, negotiated a deal whereby North Korea would stop its nuclear program in return for U.S. promises of various kinds of aid. (In 2002 North Korea was found to have gone back on its word, however.)

In 1988 Jimmy Carter and his predecessor in office, Gerald Ford, collaborated on an unusual project. They formed a team of twenty-five experts from both parties to study the challenges that would face the next president. Out of this work came a book that the two former presidents wrote, called *American Agenda: Report to the Forty-First President of the United States of America*. Full of specific recommendations for creating a more secure future, it was widely read by the American public and sent to the first President Bush. "Unfortunately," Ford joked afterward, "Bush praised our report, then never implemented any of our recommendations."

In the years following Camp David, one of the things that Carter realized was that he had made a great mistake in not inviting the Palestinians to be a part of the negotiations. Their fate was being discussed and decided in the talks between Israel and Egypt, yet they had had no voice in the process. When Carter came to understand this, he and Rosalynn traveled to meet with Palestinian leader Yasser Arafat, as well as Israeli leaders. But just when he felt he was making real progress toward some sort of peace, his hopes were dashed by the first President Bush's invasion of Iraq, Operation Desert Storm, which threw the whole region into turmoil, fear, and renewed antagonisms.

Other peace efforts were also destined to fail. Carter did not have much success when he went to try to end the terrible war in the broken and divided country of Yugoslavia, where once again neighbor was killing neighbor. Eventually things in the region fell apart so totally that NATO forces went in and bombed the country to stop the fighting. Carter was able to help very little. But he was guided by the motto he used frequently: "The worst thing that you can do is not try."

Sometimes Carter went to extremes when he was trying and ended up making controversial decisions. He became known for being willing to talk to the worst dictators, the most brutal warmongers, flattering them and hugging their wives, to get the results he wanted. Sometimes these things did not look pretty in the press. But more often than not, they worked.

Perhaps it was because of his own bad experience with a fixed election in Georgia, but one of the causes most dear to Jimmy Carter has been ensuring that elections in fragile, turbulent democracies are as free and as fair as they could possibly be. He and his team have traveled all over the world to give advice, browbeat leaders into setting up open elections, and monitor polling places. They have gone to Panama, Nicaragua, Haiti, the Dominican Republic, Jamaica, and Zambia, among others. Carter even traveled to Cuba, one of the world's last remaining Communist nations, and tried all through the 1990s to convince President Fidel

Castro to set up open elections. He failed but built a good relationship with the Cuban leader. In 2002, amid much publicity, Carter went back again and entreated both the United States and Cuba to establish better relations. His speech was televised in Cuba. "Our two nations," he said, "have been trapped in a destructive state of belligerence for forty-two years, and it is time for us to change our relationship and the way we think and talk about each other."

One of the causes with which Jimmy Carter's name is always associated is the organization called Habitat for Humanity. Its founder, a Georgia minister named Millard Fuller, started the group to build or refurbish housing for poor people in the United States and other countries. The construction is done by volunteers. Carter had heard of the group, but Fuller worked hard to get him interested, knowing that Carter was a skilled carpenter who made beautiful furniture as a hobby. Rosalynn, at first, was not sure they should be associated with what she feared was some kind of screwball group, but finally they agreed to work on a building project in Americus, Georgia, where the organization was headquartered. When Carter showed up in his blue jeans and saw how many volunteers there were, how much good they were doing, and how much fun it was, he was hooked on Habitat. Things really took off when Fuller talked Jimmy and Rosalynn into traveling by bus from Georgia to New York City with a Habitat group to help refurbish a derelict apartment building. When they arrived in New York, they were thoroughly discouraged. The building was a terrible mess, and there were not enough supplies. But gradually the project took shape, and people began to come from all over to catch a glimpse of the former president and his wife in overalls and work shoes, hammering, carrying Sheetrock, and sweating along with everyone else. The project became a media sensation and helped Habitat raise more money than it ever had before. Today Carter remains deeply involved with the group.

Through all of this global work, Carter continued to teach Sunday school at his hometown church whenever he could. But Carter broke publicly with the Southern Baptist Church in 2000, because he was unhappy with their treatment of women—particularly their ban on women becoming pastors. Carter did pledge to continue to teach Sunday school, though. "Not everyone can play in the NBA, win a Nobel Prize, or make millions in the stock market," he told his Bible class (before he won his own Nobel Prize). "But everyone can be successful according to the standards of God. Each of us can honor God through our life's commitment, in our activities, and through giving and sharing our time and talents with others."

World hunger has always been near the top of the Carter Center's to-do list as well. Through the work of its scientists, led by Nobel Prize–winning agricultural expert Norman Borlaug, the center has developed ways to ease crop shortages and end famine by developing new strains of plants. These newer breeds are able to thrive on less water and fewer nutrients and still yield four times more food than the old crops. When the Carters visited Ethiopia after the war they had done so much work to end, they were thrilled to meet farmers who had never heard of them but were growing these new crops with amazing results. They are part of what is called the green revolution.

Carter is not without his detractors. England's BBC News reports that there are some, involved with other aid groups, who feel that the former president is too prone to work unilaterally, making decisions and taking actions alone when they should be coordinated with others. There are others who feel that Carter is doing the work he does to rehabilitate the image that was so battered by his presidency. But there is no one on earth who can deny that Jimmy Carter has done an incalculable amount of good in the years since leaving the Oval Office.

Reacting to the news of Carter's Nobel Prize, fellow ex-president Bill Clinton said, "He continues to inspire people everywhere . . . through his vigorous quest for peace, justice, and a better quality of life for all citizens of the world. The Nobel Peace Prize was made for people like Jimmy Carter."

EPILOGUE ✦

REEVALUATING A PRESIDENT

Often, as time goes by after he steps down, a president's term of office begins gradually to be reassessed, sometimes for the better, sometimes for the worse. In the case of Jimmy Carter, the reassessment has been universally positive. Though he is widely acknowledged to have been a much better ex-president than president, his presidency has started looking better and better to historians and political observers.

There were a few positive voices early on. Claude Pepper, a longtime congressman from Florida, said in 1981, "As history has evaluated the administration of President Truman much higher than he was evaluated by his contemporaries, I think history will evaluate the administration of President Carter far above the evaluation of his contemporaries' administration[s]."

By 1987 even the ultraconservative senator Barry

Goldwater had to agree. "The longer [Carter] stays out of office," he said, "the better he is going to look." Political writer Anthony Lewis agreed, saying, "as historians seriously study Carter's presidency their fair-minded appraisal will add up to a big plus."

It is likely that Carter's tireless work for peace in the post-presidency years started people looking at his presidency in a different way. They began to understand that he was dead serious about peace and human rights all along. Hendrik Hertzberg, the respected writer and editor who was once Carter's speechwriter, contributed an essay on his former boss to the book *Character Above All: Ten Presidents from FDR to George Bush.* In it he said, "In Carter's case, the post-presidential career shows that his inner resources—his inner strengths—are extraordinary, far deeper than they appeared to be when he was president. Many aspects of the character people saw in him then have turned out to be obviously genuine, and some of them are perfectly suited to the work he has created for himself."

Even the episode that was the worst disaster of his term in office, the hostage crisis, is being looked at in a different way by some. Historically presidents give themselves a big boost in the polls by going to war. In Carter's situation most presidents would have done just that, especially with the public growing more and more impatient for some kind of dramatic action to prove to the world that America was not weak and pitiful. But Carter was not that kind of president. He hates war now, and he hated it then. "When the mission failed," Hertzberg says, "we all realized that we would probably lose the election. But I've thought a lot about it over the years, and to me the disaster in the desert was one of Jimmy Carter's finest hours. This was not a careless or excessive or immoral use of force. The amount of force was calibrated to the goal: freeing the hostages, and freeing them directly, as opposed to raining down indiscriminate destruction. . . . I just wish it had worked. I just wish it had worked." His assessment now is that the mission actually was a partial success, because it made the Iranians realize that the United States was willing to use force and spurred them to negotiate the release of the hostages.

When Hertzberg gets finished telling us about all

Jimmy Carter's personality flaws (and he knew them as well as anyone ever did) he gives us his final, considered verdict on the man:

"Jimmy Carter is a saint."

BIBLIOGRAPHY ★

BOOKS

Brinkley, Douglas. *The Unfinished Presidency: Jimmy Carter's Journey Beyond the White House*. New York: Viking, 1998.

Carter, Jimmy. *An Hour Before Daylight: Memories of a Rural Boyhood*. New York: Simon & Schuster, 2001.

Carter, Jimmy, and Rosalynn Carter. *Everything to Gain: Making the Most of the Rest of Your Life*. New York: Random House, 1987.

Carter, Jimmy. *Keeping Faith: Memoirs of a President*. New York: Bantam, 1983.

Foner, Eric, and John A. Garraty, eds. "Carter, Jimmy," in *The Reader's Companion to American History*. Boston: Houghton-Mifflin Company, 1991.

Hertzberg, Hendrik. "Jimmy Carter (1977–1981)," in Robert A. Wilson, ed. *Character Above All: Ten Presidents from FDR to George Bush*. New York: Simon & Schuster, 1995.

Morris, Kenneth Earl. *Jimmy Carter: American Moralist*. Athens, Georgia: University of Georgia Press, 1996.

Schraff, Anne E. *Jimmy Carter* (United States Presidents Series). Springfield, N.J.: Enslow Publishers, Inc., 1998.

Stroud, Kandy. *How Jimmy Won: The Victory Campaign from Plains to the White House*. New York: William Morrow and Company, Inc., 1977.

Wooten, James. *Dasher: The Roots and the Rising of Jimmy Carter*. New York: Summit Books, 1978.

WEB RESOURCES

Biography of Jimmy Carter:
   http://odur.let.rug.nl/~usa/P/jc39/about/jecbio.htm

Biography of Jimmy Carter:
   http://www.whitehouse.gov/history/presidents/jc39.html

The Carter Center: http://www.cartercenter.org

Interview with Jimmy Carter, American Academy of Achievement:
   http://www.achievement.org

Jimmy Carter Library and Museum: http://www.jimmycarterlibrary.org

Jimmy Carter's Inaugural Address: http://www.bartleby.com/124/pres60.html

PBS's *American President* Web site: http://www.americanpresident.org

ARTICLES

On the Web
"After the White House." BBC News: Wednesday, 21 June, 2000.
   http://news.bbc.co.uk/2/hi/americas/799949.stm

"Carter's speech to Cubans." BBC News: Wednesday, 15 May, 2002.
   http://news.bbc.co.uk/1/hi/americas/1988566.stm

"Carter to Observe Jamaica Elections." Guardian: Tuesday October 15, 2002.
   http://www.guardian.co.uk/worldlatest/story/0,1280,2089844,00.html

"Jimmy Carter splits with Baptists." BBC News: Saturday, 21 October, 2000.
   http://news.bbc.co.uk/2/hi/americas/982650.stm

"Jimmy Carter wins Nobel Peace Prize." BBC NEWS: Friday, 11 October,
   2002. http://news.bbc.co.uk/2/hi/europe/2319289.stm

"Larry King talks with Nobel-winning Carter." CNN.com: Friday, October 11, 2002.
http://www.cnn.com/2002/US/10/11/cnna.carter.king/

"Lillian Carter: Wife, Mother, and Caregiver."
http://www.sowega.net/~plainsed/research/profiles/LillianCarter.htm

"Nobel Peace Prize Laureate 2002." The Official Web Site of the Norwegian Nobel Institute, The Nobel Foundation.
http://www.nobel.no/

"Rosalynn Smith Carter."
http://www.whitehouse.gov/history/firstladies/rc39.html

Text of The Nobel Peace Prize for 2002. The Official Web Site of the Norwegian Nobel Institute,
http://www.nobel.no/eng_peace_2002.html

In print

Gettleman, Jeffrey. "Nobel Peace Prize Awarded to Carter, With Jab at Bush." *New York Times*: October 12, 2002.

Riding, Alan. "Nobel Committee Wins Praise and Criticism for Prize to Carter." *New York Times*: October 12, 2002.

"Text: Statement From Carter Accepting [Nobel] Prize." *New York Times*: October 11, 2002.

Wines, Michael. "Conflict in Oslo Over a Pointed Peace Prize." *New York Times*: October 14, 2002.